SIMPLE
SHORTS

Judy Flohr

Trafford
PUBLISHING™

Although some of these stories are based upon real events and real characters, the author has made every effort to fictionalize them while maintaining the integrity of the work.

Order this book online at www.trafford.com/07-1827
or email orders@trafford.com

Most Trafford titles are also available at major online book retailers.

Note for Librarians: A cataloguing record for this book is available from Library and Archives Canada at www.collectionscanada.ca/amicus/index-e.html

Printed in Victoria, BC, Canada.

ISBN: 978-1-4251-4362-6

We at Trafford believe that it is the responsibility of us all, as both individuals and corporations, to make choices that are environmentally and socially sound. You, in turn, are supporting this responsible conduct each time you purchase a Trafford book, or make use of our publishing services. To find out how you are helping, please visit www.trafford.com/responsiblepublishing.html

Our mission is to efficiently provide the world's finest, most comprehensive book publishing service, enabling every author to experience success. To find out how to publish your book, your way, and have it available worldwide, visit us online at www.trafford.com/10510

 www.trafford.com

North America & international
toll-free: 1 888 232 4444 (USA & Canada)
phone: 250 383 6864 ♦ fax: 250 383 6804 ♦ email: info@trafford.com

The United Kingdom & Europe
phone: +44 (0)1865 722 113 ♦ local rate: 0845 230 9601
facsimile: +44 (0)1865 722 868 ♦ email: info.uk@trafford.com

10 9 8 7 6 5 4

Imagination was given to man to compensate him for what he is not; a sense of humor to console him for what he is.

= Francis Bacon

Contents

SHORT SHORTS

Virginia Gentleman

THE VIRGINIA GENTLEMAN OWNS what used to be called a plantation. I think he just calls the land he inherited "a horse farm" now, even though he raises cows, chickens, and children right along with the horses.

His acreage elegantly supports not only a large, old, brick mansion with columns marching around its porches, but barns, outbuildings, meadows, pastures, ponds and woods. His wife plants and tends a lush garden between the gravel drive and the back porch. It shouts fertility and glory with many varieties of vegetables, herbs, roses and tall stately sunflowers. Their thin stalks erupt into color and fullness, reminding me of skinny brown-faced folks with huge, smiling faces, like those pictures of the sun shining we all drew when we were children.

His wife once brought a Belted Galloway calf, still soft and fuzzy but quite ill from being purchased too early, into her home during the winter. Its bulk blocked the roaring fire in the parlor. She fed it from a baby bottle while the ancestors peered down sternly from their gold-gilded frames. They frowned, but said nothing. Of course, the calf thrived with all that warmth and cooing care and now comes up to her in the pasture and nuzzles her arms for strokes and hugs. His name is Bugsy. I doubt if they'll ever be able to eat him.

The Virginia gentleman can ride a horse, jump a horse, breed a horse and, believe it or not, is an equine insurance broker. He spends less time insuring horses now that slavery has been abolished, and his parcel of land is very large. He does, however, attend horse races from Foxfield to Middleburg and even as far away as Saratoga. "I can only stay for the races," he says. "That place is just too far north for me."

Tromping through the vast tangle of empty farmland in early fall with Maker's Mark breath, shotguns, and jumpy hound dogs, he is an educated hunter. His friends accompany him. The sound of their gunshots and shouts of manly joy can be heard for as much as half a mile. Although adept at foxhunting astride his horse, he prefers shooting coons. "Coons can climb trees, and the better hidden the prey, the more challenge to put a bullet in it. Foxhunts are for women."

Now, shotguns and rifles aside, this gentleman can sling a handgun faster than an old western hero.

"Don't ever let anyone tell you that if you have black snakes around, you won't have copperheads. Roland and I were spreading a bale of hay out in the barn, and damn if a huge black snake didn't jump right out at us. With the next poke, we found a mother copperhead giving birth. They don't lay eggs, you know. These suckers were being born alive. I whipped out my pistol and shot every last one of them," he says. Who can blame him?

A comely fellow, he has a shock of light brown hair that falls perfectly over his eyes, which always look directly at folks, especially when he shakes their hands. His children have been taught to do the same. Their comfort in the presence of adults is a trait much admired in the south. "Those children are certainly gracious and well-bred," is a circulating remark at each of their social gatherings.

Speaking of social gatherings, the Virginia gentleman will present his daughter into society when she is twenty-one. She will join other lovely, perfectly mannered, and properly educated young ladies as they descend the stairs at the Club in stunning, long white dresses and long white gloves on the arms of their tuxedo-clad fathers, who will also be wearing gloves.

One might get a glimpse of the Virginia gentleman's cummerbund as he lifts his arm so his daughter can slip her arm into his. Waving proudly atop his taut waistline will be a circling army of embroidered tiny confederate flags.

Although it is likely these striking virgins have

consumed large amounts of vodka before their dainty descent, they can now openly and proudly raise their glasses in front of family and close friends.

This memorable debutante ball will be the beginning of full social status and legal drinking, and the end of stocking the tampon machine in the ladies room with miniature airline bottles of liquor—an art each one perfected at the tender age of fifteen.

"No more having to call the best defense lawyers and right judges in the middle of the night," the Virginia gentleman laughs, and his counterparts drink a toast. It is, indeed, a Kodak moment, and the professional photographer who has been entrusted with this high honor will make sure it is a coming out like no other.

As you probably have guessed, the Virginia gentleman's children will both attend his own alma mater. "As far as I'm concerned," he says as if he's joking, "there are no schools above the Mason-Dixon line." His legacy at The University is a long one. More importantly, an old family friend has given said school a fine, new, made to look very old, brick building. And I, like Bugsy, love to immerse myself in the warmth and charm of the Virginia gentleman's companionship.

Waiting

THE DOOR FINALLY OPENED. Out stepped a very fat lady wearing a white uniform and sturdy white shoes. Even her stockings were white. They did not hide her hairy legs.

"Keep it down out here!" she yelled at all of us. "The building is shaking. Next."

Two miniature poodles stopped twirling and trotted toward the door. One was silver and one was baby blue. Their toenails clicked on the tile floor. Their tutus were made of pink netting.

We had been waiting and waiting. I was thinking about waiting. Then I stopped to see if I could feel the building shaking. A clown sat near the door where the fat nurse had just poked out her puffy face.

"My toe hurts," he said. "I think those pesky midgets broke it during their march."

We all looked at his huge, purple leather clown shoes. Sure enough, his large right toe was sticking through the front end of his left shoe. It had even poked a hole in his red and white striped stocking. It looked swollen. So did his feet. A tear rolled down his white painted face and his big red smile melted into a frown.

"It is probably only sprained," the ringmaster sitting next to him leaned down and squinted at the toe. He cracked his whip on the floor. "Yep, just sprained."

Two elephants stood beside the water cooler looking out the window. They were shifting their weight and whispering. A stately man in a black three-piece suit sat nearby. Red, gold, green and blue silk handkerchiefs peeked from his vest pocket.

"Why don't you wash the windows while you wait?" I asked the elephants.

They looked at one another. "Good idea," the smaller one said. He lifted the top off the water cooler and dipped his trunk into it. Then he squirted a window. The other one snatched the gold silk handkerchief from the magician's vest and wiped the window dry. They washed and wiped. Their big rear ends jiggled along.

"Watch out!" the magician shouted. "That kerchief is magic!" He jumped up and tried to grab it from the larger elephant. Two rabbits fell from his pants leg. They scurried around the clown's sore toe.

"Ouch!" the clown shouted.

When the magician got down on his knees and

tried to scoop the rabbits up into his top hat, his wand fell from his hand. It rattled and rolled across the floor. A tiger in the chair next to me jabbed at it with his paw.

"Don't touch that!" I yelled to the tiger. "We might all disappear."

The tiger poked at it anyway. He looked at me and rolled his eyes. Then he swished his big striped tail and knocked me out of my chair. I landed on the floor with a thud.

"Oh my," said the man riding around the room on his unicycle. "Let me help you." He reached over to pull me up and a rabbit ran right in front of him. His bike fell over. It lay with its big wheel spinning and spinning. The rabbit stopped and looked at both of us sitting on the floor. Then it scurried under the tiger's chair.

The unicycle man picked up the magic wand and played a tune on the spinning spokes. The elephants turned around and began to dance to the music. One window was still smudged.

The door opened and the fat woman in white burst through. A tiny brightly colored car zoomed down the hallway behind her and roared into the waiting room. It went right between her fat hairy legs and screeched to a stop in the middle of the room. The two little poodles came prancing out behind it. They sat down and fluffed their tutus. They crossed their legs.

The big nurse looked around the room. She was frowning. "I told all of you to hold it down!" she shouted. Then she looked at the floor. Under each chair sat a bunny.

"Where did all these rabbits come from?" No one said a word. A ray of sun glinted off the tiny fender of the miniature car. She raised her head, "And how in the world did you guys get the windows so clean?"

Bliss

"Hey, can't you get a beer in here? I don't see one person with a drink." I grabbed Jim's arm as we looked around "Daze in the Park," the downtown club we had just tunneled our way into. Laser lights bounced their beams off a black floor with mirrored walls, where baggy pants, nose rings, halter tops, and even goggles duplicated their images everywhere. Lined up along the walls were what appeared to be hundreds of water bottles. Some people even had them hanging on chains around their necks.

"No, I told you, this is a rave club. People do X, not alcohol," he whispered back to me."

"Okay, I'm cool with that. I just thought they'd at least serve beer—for those of us who have no aversion to the good ol' boy drug of choice."

Using X had no appeal for me, but I agreed to

join my old college buddy, Jim, just to see this cultish underground scene that promises mind liberation, being awash with waves of love and peace, and profound self-knowledge—only the good kind. I hadn't quite figured out how someone could be so immersed in a hunger for deep empathy and sensory awareness. Jim had popped his pill on the way down here.

"Let's go out back," I said, noticing a long hallway leading to a lighted patio.

"I gotta dance first," Jim said and headed to the middle of the floor, where, by now, serious techno music had molded crowds of goggled, pierced, young folks into a bobbing throb of up and down movement. No one danced with anyone other than themselves but sure enough, they were all smiling at one another and being extremely careful not to jar other bobbers. I laughed, headed for the patio alone. Or so I thought.

As I turned around, a young girl dressed in a long, flowing skirt with what appeared to be fluorescent paw prints on it caught me gently by the shoulders and began a slow, tender, neck rub.

"There, how does that feel?" she asked me.

"Fine, thank you. Excuse me, I'm headed out back."

"Okay, peace to you," she gave me a beatific smile. I continued on.

"Hey, you want an X?" a tall, dark, dreadlocked youth without a shirt smiled a huge white-toothed smile right into my face.

"Uh, no thanks," I stammered and nudged my way toward the back door.

"I am overcome with unity and respect," a pretty blond smiled at me, her cigarette dropping ashes from her lips as she reached up and touched my forehead.

"And I am overcome with heat and physical contact," I replied, touching her forehead in return.

I finally made it to the patio door and thankful for a little cool air, took a lungful as I stepped out. A group of X'ers was sitting in a circle around a bongo drum, smiling and chatting with one another. It had the familial feel of a reunion of long lost loved ones, reuniting and bonding. A pony-tailed man watched me breathing fresh air, walked over and grinned, "That's the way, brother, take it all in. Let the oxygen unite with X. It enhances the release of your brain's serotonin."

"Well, that's good," I said, sincerely and bravely. "What's the downside?"

"Are you kidding? There is no downside. Are you like a narc, or something?" He was still smiling. "Just drink a lot of water. You did bring water, didn't you?"

I didn't wish to alarm him, so I just smiled and then turned around. When I gingerly shoved my way back down the hallway, Jim was nowhere in sight. Not that I could see him anyway. Dodging bodies on the floor required my eyes be directed downward. Were they dead? Had they passed out? No, when the colored lasers flashed over them, I could see that they were hugging, laughing, and rolling around the polished black floor. I think their positive energy was in overdrive, a hot, cooing, spiritually blitzed mass of sweaty bodies, sharing insights and bottled water.

I kindly made my way out, nodding and grinning to those still on their feet, turned on the street and headed for Bud's, my favorite pool hall and beer joint. There, I knew I would feel that blind universal love without swallowing anything other than a tall, cold beer. And sure enough, the billiard balls on Bud's blinking neon sign beckoned benevolently and in I went.

My spiritual journey had begun. Large, muscled, tattooed, plaid-shirted truck drivers were molded into barstools, most of them accompanied by big-breasted beauties hoisting pastel drinks and laughing without pretense. Several folks were singing and raising their glasses along to Kenny Chesney as he droned from the old blinking Wurlitzer in the corner, "When the sun goes down...it'll be all right..." Joyful faces turned toward me as I stepped up to the bar. I sensed goodness, generosity.

"Hey there, friend, how the hell are you doing? What'll you have?" Bud hollered.

"I will have spiritual enlightenment, with a twist of grace and a splash of reality."

Everyone laughed. A big guy on the stool next to me rolled his eyes, wiped his forehead with the sleeve of his t-shirt, and then put his arm gently around my shoulders.

"Pour him a tall, cold one. Quick!" he yelled to Bud. "And I'm buyin'!"

Oldies

GEORGE HOLLY DIDN'T HEAR the cars, their horns blaring. He didn't hear the screeching brakes of the huge city bus crossing the same intersection at that exact moment. Popping from his ear, the tiny iPod speaker landed on the street next to George's head and continued to blast music from the 60's and 70's, Abba's "Listen to the Music" sending up its strains through the shouting and screaming of passers-by who witnessed the accident.

The iPod was a Father's Day gift to George, not from his children, who would have offered up organic bean soup mix or Deepak Chopra's latest quantum alternative solution to growing old and losing one's mind.

No, it was a gift from his grandchildren, ten and eight, who were enlightened enough to know both how to manipulate this little recording miracle and how much their dear grandpapa needed music in his life. They had heard him singing along to the oldies station when he drove them to their soccer games, and the volume he produced, along with the twinkle in his eyes, provided them with proof that he did, indeed, *love tunes*.

That these two kindhearted children took the time to teach him to download his blasts from the past, was further indication to him the new generation was not without compassion.

"That poor man," people said aloud when they saw his head hit the pavement. The bus driver was distraught.

"I never saw him," he lamented and the gathering crowed let out a unified "Aah," sharing solidarity of his dilemma but really sending forth a prayer of thanksgiving that it was not them who had been driving.

A brightly colored hot air balloon floated down to the scene. The Fifth Dimension jumped out, dressed in bright orange EMT jumpsuits. "Would you like to ride in our beautiful balloon?" one of them asked George, shaking his shoulder. George became responsive.

He smiled up at them but before he could answer, Janis Joplin strolled over. In one hand she held a nearly empty bottle of Jim Beam. In the other, a small red heart, thumping to a beat.

"Here, George," she slurred in her raspy voice, "take another little piece of my heart." He did.

Holding it tightly to his chest, he was lifted onto a stretcher and the last sight he had on the street as he was being loaded onto the beautiful balloon was Marilyn Monroe, standing over the subway grate, trying unsuccessfully to hold down her billowing white chiffon dress. She pursed her lips at him and winked with her already half closed eye.

"Happy Birthday, Mr. Folly," she mouthed seductively, then took her hand off her skirt and blew him a full lipped kiss.

The craft lifted up, hissing and swaying. Grace Slick leaned over him, her breasts pouring out of a white nurse's uniform. She held something out to him. Oh yes, it was a handful of colorful pills, big ones, small ones, pills of all shapes and sizes.

"One pill makes you larger, one pill makes you small," she sang. "Which one do you want, Georgie?"

"All of them," he answered. He reached for the pills.

"Don't take all of them," shouted several voices. "You'll be dazed and confused." George looked around and saw Led Zeppelin perched on the edge of the beautiful balloon.

"Oh, okay," George smiled up at them, reached only for the yellow one, popped it into his mouth. "Where are we going, by the way? And where is my iPod?"

"I think it is still on the street," said Bruce Springsteen, who was sitting on a box in the beautiful balloon, strumming his guitar. "But don't worry, I was 'Born to Run' so when we land, I will go get it."

"Thank you!" said George. "Will you play us a few tunes while we are floating around up here? Where are we going, by the way?"

Bruce nodded, began strumming and playing "Streets of Philadelphia." George closed his eyes. "Good, that's where I live."

When the song ended and George looked up again, Jimi Hendrix was at the controls.

"Are you experienced?" George hollered at him.

"Well, I am in sort of a 'Purple Haze' up here but Mick just told us to 'get off his cloud' so I will navigate to earth the best I can." Jimi shook his bushy head and laughed.

The balloon began shaking and spinning around. "Just 'Stand by Me!'" shouted B.B. King. George sat up and looked for B.B., but the balloon was nowhere to be seen.

His wife Marge was leaning over him, peering intently into his face.

"George, you're awake! Thank goodness. Dr. Lennon said you had a concussion and were probably just 'watching the wheels go round and round' and that we should be patient. Dr. Lennon!" Marge ran to the hall, looked both ways, then returned to George's bedside. "He must have left."

"He'll be back." George smiled up at Marge. "I wanna hold your hand."

Marge took his hand. "Oh, George, the police-woman said that a great-looking guy in tight jeans and a leather jacket turned in your iPod. She said he was 'hot' and carrying a guitar. Apparently he pulled

up on a big motorcycle just after the accident."
"Well, good," said George. "I must add more
tunes. For now, I will just rest. InAGaddaDaVida."
Then he closed his eyes.

Burma Shave

Rose Ann Martin watched in disbelief as her brother Bobby casually tossed one of her favorite blue sneakers out of the car window. He just grabbed it off the seat beside her and tossed it right out. She had pulled them off her feet just minutes earlier and laid them carefully beside her when the July sun began beating down through the rear window, making the back seat unbearably hot, despite the windows being rolled all the way down. The wind was hot, too. It blew Rose Ann's hair loose from the rubber bands her mother had twisted around her pigtails early that morning.

"Your new blue sneakers will be so pretty with your new blue and white checked sundress," her mother told her. "Just be sure and put on your ruffled white socks with them. Grandma is going to be so happy to see you and Bobby."

Now they were speeding down the two lane country road. Rose Ann was hot and sticky, her hair was
tickling her face, and Bobby had just thrown her
shoe out the window!

"Mommeeeeeee," she wailed, "Bobby just threw
my new sneaker out of the car!"

"WHAT!" Her mother turned around and looked
at her. The rolled-down windows had blown her
blonde curly hair everywhere, too, and her face was
red and dripping little drops beneath her nose. Her
voice was loud, and Rose Ann knew her mother's
"What!" meant that she did not really want to know
what. She yelled it again anyway, hoping to be heard
over the wind whipping everywhere in the scorching
car.

"My sneaker, Bobby just threw it out the
window!"

"Ed, stop the car and turn around!" Mrs. Martin
hollered at her husband. Bobby sat quietly in his
corner of the back seat, squinting out the open window, staring at the dry rattling cornfields flying by.
His hair wasn't blowing. He had a crew cut. He even
looked cool, not a patch of sweat anywhere on his
chubby, freckled face or red and blue striped t-shirt.
His high-top black sneakers were tied safely on
his feet, which were crossed at the ankles and just
reached the floor. His chin rested on his hand, which
was propped on his elbow, firmly rooted on the arm-
rest of the door.

Their father stopped and pulled off to the side of
the road. Dust rose and gravel crunched and spit.

There they were, sitting in front of the first of five red and white Burma Shave signs. It said, "Don't lose your head...." Rose Ann looked down the road to read the second one, but the dust hadn't settled.

"Now, what did you say?" Her mother was angry.

"Bobby threw my shoe out the window." Rose Ann lowered her voice this time. Her mother glared at her brother.

"Bobby, why did you do that? How far back? What in the world is wrong with you? Ed, turn around. We'll have to drive back and look for it."

"I didn't throw her stupid ol' blue sneaker out of the window!" Bobby argued, rolling his eyes, and scrunching up his face. "She did it herself. It just went out the window on its way by my head, which is what she was aiming at. I can't help it that she missed." He gave his mother a sweet smile. "But, thank goodness she did miss. That woulda hurt."

Ed Martin looked in the rearview mirror and reversed direction with a quickly executed three-point turn. Now they were going back the way they had just come. All three of them were straining their necks out the open windows looking for the sneaker. Not Rose Ann, though. She sat quietly in her corner, watching them, hearing the silence, knowing that it was Bobby they believed. They always did. Why bother trying to tell them? She could feel tears behind her eyes, so she closed them as tight as she could to keep them from sliding out.

"There it is!" her father shouted. "Right in the middle of the lane over there. Wow, we were lucky a car didn't come along and run over it." He spoke too soon.

A huge semi appeared out of nowhere, bearing down on the sneaker at what seemed like a hundred miles an hour. Before Mr. Martin could even put the gear in park, it thundered past them, rocking their sedan and blasting hot steamy exhaust in all their faces.

"Oh, sh..." his voice was drowned out by the roaring truck. He continued to climb out, left the door open and ran quickly over to the shoe. It was squished flat.

"It's flattened!" His voice got higher, and Rose Ann thought for a second he was going to cry, too. He didn't. He just picked it up like a wounded bird and tried to fluff it back up by sticking his free hand inside it and moving it around. No luck. He walked over to the car and handed it through the window to Rose Ann. She took it from him, pulled up her white-ruffled stockinged foot, and tried to jam it back in the collapsed sneaker. It really was flat and as she struggled to force her foot back in it, she still tried not to cry.

Her father watched her, hands on his hips. His baggy polyester short-sleeved shirt had come untucked from his belted, loose-fitting trousers. He was frowning and looked older and madder than Rose Ann had seen him.

"Serves you right, Rose Ann, if you walk lopsided all afternoon at Grandma's. You know better than to throw things at your brother. And now we'll have to buy a new pair."

He shook his head, slid into the front seat, put the car in gear, checked the rearview mirror and pulled slowly back into the other lane. They were again on their way. Rose Ann said nothing. Bobby grinned at her, licked his pointing finger, and traced a line in the air. "One more for me," he whispered.

They were passing the Burma Shave signs again now. Rose Ann began reading them to herself. "Don't lose your head..." "To gain a minute…" "You need your head…" Your brains are in it." Bobby read them, too, and then looked at Rose Ann.

"Don't worry, Bobby, about *your* head. That's not where *your* brains are. You don't have any." She laughed, licked her finger and drew a line in the air.

Goblins

JUST AS NONIE'S MOTHER turns out her blue bunny lamp and pulls her bedroom door almost closed, the way Nonie likes it, a goblin peeks out of her closet. He's early tonight, thinks Nonie, staring into his twinkling red eyes. She lifts her hand from under the soft blue polka dot quilt and waves. He grins back, huge greenish yellow teeth turning upwards. Her mother's footstep noises fade away down the carpeted hallway.

"It's okay. She's gone. Come on out. Why are you in such a hurry tonight?" she whispers.

"My toe hurts," the goblin says, gliding over and sitting on her bed. He pulls his foot up and props it carefully beside her

"Which one?" Nonie leans over and peers intently. "You only have three."

"It's this one, the middle one," he sighs.

"Well, what should we do? Does this mean we don't get to travel tonight?" she asks.

"Does your mommy have something to make it feel better?" he asks hopefully. He knows how disappointed they both will be if they can't have their nightly adventure.

Nonie thinks for a moment. "Well, she has this greasy stuff that is supposed to kill germs. Knee a soarin' or something like that. We'll have to wait until she's asleep though."

"I don't see germs, do you?" the goblin asks. He and Nonie both inspect his toe, their brows wrinkling. "Besides, I don't want to kill anything!" he sounds alarmed.

Nonie laughs out loud, then covers her mouth with her hands so her mother won't hear her. She touches his middle toe lightly. She pulls up his foot and turns it over, looking hard at the other side.

"Did you bend it funny or did it get stepped on?" she asks.

The goblin scrunches his face, ponders the question. "No, I don't think so. Not that I can remember. I love your new black shiny shoes, by the way."

"Oh, my new Sunday ones, black patent leather with the gold buckle?"

"Yes, they're wonderful."

"I am so glad you like them. I picked them out myself."

Nonie's eyes open wide. "Oh dear, did you try them on while you were waiting in my closet?" She looks up at the goblin expectantly.

"I sure did. I really like them. I hope you don't mind. They didn't fit though."

"Mind?" Nonie giggles, "Of course I don't mind, you silly ol'goblin. Now we know what's wrong with your toe."

"We do?" he tilts his head, and his red eyes grow large and round.

"Sure. You must have jammed it when you tried on my new shoes. It'll feel better soon."

"It will? Oh, good!" He lowered his foot to the floor and wiggled his toes. "It feels a little better already! Now where should we fly tonight? He crosses his legs and puts his hands on his chin. The playground? I like to swing. The park? We could take a spin on the carousel. I got it! Let's fly over to the ocean. You know how much I love watching the moon make shapes on the waves. They remind me of my family." He sighs.

"Let's do that!" Nonie says, "Watching the moon play on the ocean will make you feel better. Thinking about your family will get your mind off your sore toe!"

Nonie pulls back her blue checked curtains and looks up at the sky. "It's a full one tonight, too!"

Over The Edge

MOONLIGHT SPLINTERED THROUGH THE lace curtains as they billowed softly in the nighttime breeze, playing at the open bedroom window. A middle-aged woman in a double bed awoke suddenly, her heart pounding in terror. Even though every nerve in her trembling body was electrified, it took a laborious effort to sit up.

"Oh, God," she thought, "What is going on with me?" She glanced at the empty space in the bed next to her. No, that wasn't it. Her husband of twenty years was gone now, leaving her widowed and facing alone several years of their son's agonizing crack cocaine addiction. Her clock read 3:32 a.m. The neon green numbers stared blankly into the dark. Yes, that was it. He hadn't come home yet. She would have heard the door open.

"Please, Lord," she whispered. "Let him be okay—asleep on the grungy floor of a drug buddy's apartment and not winding his way stoned or high through the snarling (even in the wee hours) traffic on the Los Angeles freeways."

The woman had imagined it a thousand times— the police at the door, her own voice screeching in horror as the sheet was slowly pulled back from the body on the slab at the morgue, the smell of the damp brown earth as his coffin was lowered into it.

Yes, she knew that addiction could split apart the very foundation of one's life, leaving every layer exposed to endless questions and examinations. The counselor at rehab told her to attend meetings, which she had been doing for months.

She sat through those meetings week after week, feeling the pain of other parents as they laid bare their hearts, looking for relief. She tried desperately to work the steps, take her own inventory, and let God handle it for her. Changing her contempt for her son's actions, respecting the potential she knew was within him—it was the only way. She could see herself leaving an addicted spouse, but a son? Her only child? Weren't mothers supposed to care for and protect their offspring? She just couldn't absorb the part about letting him "hit bottom" when she could well imagine the bottom being death.

No, even though she was aware she had spent years teetering on the brink of insanity—lecturing, moralizing, threatening—she still had a shred of hope.

Sometimes she saw herself—her very soul—a piece of debris being propelled down a mountain in water from a winter snow melt—unbridled and violent and totally unable to avoid the inevitable devastating destruction that would follow. These images always ended in the so familiar prayer, "God, grant me the serenity to accept…"

The blaring ring of the doorbell pierced through the "wisdom to know the difference." She quickly wiped her tears, threw on the old blue bathrobe at the foot of her bed, and ran out of her room. "He's home," she told herself. "He must have forgotten his key." As her mind struggled to protect her, reality crashed through, pushing her to the edge of that precipice of hell from which there would be no return. Even before she could get to the front door, the strobe of flashing blue lights danced through the hall, lighting up her tear-stained face and reflecting the total anguish upon it.

KFC

BOBBY DID NOT START Barnes Realty. His grandfather did though, and his own father has taken it over with the expectation that Bobby will someday do the same. Bobby has no desire to do this. He wants to sky dive full time. In fact, he is sitting in the front office of his family's realty office looking at a mahogany bookcase where twenty three brass parachutist trophies sit, three of them atop his newest MLS catalogue.

Spring has arrived in Sandwich, Illinois, and Bobby swivels his brown leather chair around to face the window and smiles at the clouds floating by.

"Bobby, line two," his secretary's scratchy voice rouses him. He straightens his head, rolls his chair up to the desk and frowns at the intercom.

"Bobby Barnes, may I help you?

"Bobby, how's the ol' sky flier himself?" an over-enthusiastic male voice bellows.

"This ol' sky flier is just fine. Who the hell is this?"

"Bobby, my boy, this is your lucky day! I have an offer you're gonna love! My name is Peter Duncan and I am chief marketing officer here at KFC."

"KFC as in Kentucky Fried Chicken?" Bobby asks.

"You got it! The one and only! We want you to do a little PR job for us, but first, I must have your word that whether or not you choose to be one of our fall guys, you will not divulge our plan. We are counting on the surprise of the decade here, and we don't want to give it away beforehand."

"Go on." Bobby was always hearing crazy schemes—skydivers landing on roofs of used cars, or on top of trampolines that would bounce them back up again and again. One jilted husband had even asked Bobby to land on the local Motel 6 where he was sure his wife was having an encounter. The plan concluded with trapping the unsuspecting couple in bed under the parachute.

"We want you to be a FLYING COLONEL!" Mr. Duncan was excited. "We are introducing five, I mean FIVE, can you believe it, all new chicken sand-wiches—Tender Roast, Triple Crunch, Triple Crunch Zinger, Original Recipe, and Honey BBQ! And we want you for ... are you ready? TRIPLE CRUNCH ZINGER!!! That is, it will be printed on your para-chute. We already have commitments from four of your nearest and dearest friends—Tom Singer, Gordon Davis, Joel Parker, and Austin Buerlin—and we hope you will agree to join them!!" Bobby nods at each name, imagining them plowing skillfully through the clouds.

"You mean, it's a bird, it's a plane, it's Colonel Sanders? That kind of thing?"

"You got it! Each of you will be dressed in white, white jumpsuits that is, and have a black string tie around your necks. We'll dye your hair pure white—with temporary dye, of course—and apply a fake triangle goatee with super glue so it won't fly off. And, under your goggles ... big black rimmed glasses with just frames! Each one of you will have the name of one of our new sandwiches on your chute, and you will be eating one as you come down. After your chute opens, of course! Oh, and you all will unfurl a huge red and white flag with our logo. You know it, I'm sure—it has the famous man himself on it. We will take the concept of chicken to new heights!" Bobby had to hold the phone away from his ear.

"So, you want five flying colonels to jump out of an airplane holding a logo banner, opening a chute, and eating a sandwich at the same time?"

"Yep, isn't that GREAT? We will have samples of the five fabulous sandwiches, thousands of them, to hand out to the crowds below after you land. Then all you guys can work the crowd saying things like, 'we had to pluck 'em out of thin air, you can get yours at a drive-thru.' Our creative folks are working on this now."

"And we get to do all this while trying to keep chicken grease off those white suits and keep those string ties from strangling us or smacking us in the face on the way down? Not to mention choking on a loose goatee or dropping a chicken sandwich in flight? I'LL DO IT!"

Bobby pulls his rip cord, then reaches into his pocket and extracts his Triple Crunch Zinger. He holds firmly to the banner with his other hand and looks around at his four colonel friends. Their formation is going nicely, perfectly, in fact. He bites into the Zinger. A fiery blend of peppers and spices, crispy fried chicken, lettuce, tomato, and mayonnaise tingle his mouth. "This is why it's called a Zinger!" he shouts into the air, looking down at thousands of tiny upturned faces.

His teeth are dry he is grinning so broadly. Suddenly he hears a booming jubilant chorus of voices, its chant climbing skyward in perfect rhythm: "DAMN GOOD CHICKEN! ... DAMN GOOD CHICKEN! ... DAMN GOOD CHICKEN! ..."

Marilyn

How DID IT FEEL to know that your body radiated sensuality? That every breathing male desired you? That you were a love goddess in a physique so luscious a photographer once said he had never photographed such flesh?

Did you realize you made every other woman live earthbound by comparison? Yet somehow you remained free of guile, never giving the impression you truly understood the adoration or appeal you inspired.

A pucker or pout of your full, moist, red lips and those blue eyes closed halfway, enchanted, seduced. Was there a man alive who did not wish to be in that steam vent looking up when your billowy, white, full-skirted dress blew up and about, tickling your shapely long legs while you merely threw back your head and giggled? Had those legs been sculpted in the finest Italian marble, David would cover his own.

How could every move you made be so bewitching? Every note you sang be so breathy? Each line you uttered so caressing? Each hip you thrust so inviting? Did your sexual image haunt your husbands?

People who knew you said you could make every male in a room feel like he was the one you wanted to leave with, and each one must have imagined you writhing and moaning underneath him. Yet each one must have longed to protect you, care gently for you. Were you aware of your complicated essence, your infusion of purity and innocence with lust and longing?

You told everyone you belonged to the world because you never belonged to anyone else, having been raised in orphanages and foster homes. And that you believed sex was part of nature and you adored nature, evoking with your words both carnality and divinity.

Unlike beauties today, you manifested voluptuousness, opulence, effervescence. Your breasts were lush, your hips ample and full, you radiated pure delight in being feminine. We glorify gauntness now—bony, pierced body parts exposed in fashions that make one's sex unidentifiable. Sexuality seems to have lost its joy, its mystique, its delicacy. It has become blatant and bizarre.

And how did your body finalize its enticing existence on this earth? Were narcotics pulsing so rapidly through your veins that your heart just stopped beating? Or were you murdered, done in to ensure silence about affairs with prominent political figures of the time? How ironic that is now.

Death took your body but left you the greatest gift of all—eternal youth. Untouched you shall always be by the purge of our existence here on earth—aging and the tawdriness it bestows upon human bodies. Could you have looked in a mirror as you aged and been as enchanted with what was staring back at you as you were with the movies, calendars and photographs of your youth?

Gravity would have pulled your perky breasts toward your feet, probably by way of a bulging tummy. Your taut round behind would widen and sag, atop thighs that were dimpled and dented. How would you have felt about those companions of unwanted flesh who chose to accompany your waistline, hanging on and bouncing freely, regardless of how little you ate?

How frustrated would you have been when your sexy heavy lidded look became permanent, and you had trouble finding your eyelids to enhance with eyeliner? Would you have been disgusted to see your lovely translucent skin hanging in loose folds under your chin, and heavy jowls, full and settling in, where cheek bones used to live? Could you have maintained your dignity in a culture that no longer cherishes aging women, much less full-figured aging women?

You are dignified in death. You are forever honored with vitality, youth, a body that still evokes lust and tenderness, and a body that will always enrapture, beguile and charm. Never will you be saddened or discouraged by the slouching, sagging, drooping betrayal of your earthly form. Though an earthly radiance is quelled upon this earth, nothing can diminish you.

Cheap Red Wine

A GLASS OF RED WINE. Not a Chateau Mouton Rothschild '71, or even an '82. Not a fine Napa Valley merlot like Duckhorn. Just plain red wine floating in an ordinary wine glass. Not a fine crystal Bordeaux glass, large globed and full bowled, making the taster smile and smack his lips as he twirls and watches red wine cling, syrupy and seductive, to its sparkling sides. No, just plain red wine in a plain small wine glass, waiting to be consumed by noisy wedding guests whose teeth will turn purple, announcing their choice of alcoholic beverage to everyone with whom they will make small talk. A glass of red wine.

❦

"What would you like?" the young bartender looks up at us. His face is damp. His white starched sleeves are rolled to his elbows and a black bow tie droops a bit below his smooth chin.

"We'll have red wine," my friend Karen, standing next to me, answers for both of us. He pours two glasses, picks up two small white napkins, the names Hunter and Martha Rae Wellington, III, entwined in gold print, and hands us our wine, one glass at a time.

We sip. Karen cringes, holds her glass up and squints.

"When will people stop serving such thin tinny red wine at parties? God, it's thin." she says to no one in particular. "Here, hold this."

I take her glass from her and stare into it, expecting to see pieces of tin or some tiny, mysterious diet pill.

"Well, we all can't have good taste in wine. An old, mellow Bordeaux at a wedding reception?" But she isn't listening. She is pawing through her dainty black satin shoulder bag looking, I expect, for her cigarettes. The wind picks up, rattling the outdoor tent against its poles. Our hair is blowing across our faces, hers obscured anyway as she leans further and further over, finally retrieving a Virginia Slim and placing it between her lips. I long to reach up; fasten a tickling lock behind my ear.

"Take your wine now," I hold out her glass, but she turns to a man standing beside her.

"Could I have a light, please?" The cigarette dangles from her mouth as she taps him on his shoulder. He turns suddenly, his elbow bumping hers. They both stumble a bit. I take a quick step back.

She's smoking now, laughing at something the man is telling her. He lights up, too, cupping his hand over his lighter as the wind continues to scatter tiny engraved napkins and lift flimsy flowered pastel skirts.

I finish my wine. She turns back to me, retrieves her glass and takes my arm. "Let's go talk to the happy couple. Just keep me away from Anthony." We jostle our way through tuxedoes and silk.

"Don't tell me you guys are still fighting."

"No, we aren't fighting. I just don't speak to him." Anthony is married to her husband's sister.

"You know, don't you, that you make simple things, like breathing for instance, impossible for anyone who's within twenty feet of you two? We're old bats now; we're supposed to let go of hard feelings when we flush our last Tampax. Aren't you over all that, whatever *all that* was? I can't even remember."

"You know what 'all that' was. You are *not* losing your memory, you old hag." She steers me on, her wine sloshing in her glass. We maneuver through the crowd. She follows her feet, like reading a road map tacked to the bent grass. I manage to plunk my empty glass on a small, white-clothed table as we hurry past.

We climb slowly up the hill where the bride and groom are beginning their descent toward the crowded tent from the white-columned country club porch. We look up at them walking toward us, and see that the bride's veil has blown across the groom's face. The harder he slaps at it, the more he entangles himself. She's oblivious, smiling out at her adoring crowd from atop the hill.

I turn around, hoping to spot Anthony in the crowd before Karen does. The tent looks like a huge, white hot air balloon, its basket crammed with fluttering penguins and flowers, awaiting lift off.

A crash of thunder announces the rain seconds before large drops pelt the sloping lawn. The bride and groom have broken into a stumbling run down the hill. She pulls him along. He is still swatting at her veil.

"Come on," I say. "We'll congratulate them later."

"Wait, there he is," Karen says. And sure enough, Anthony is loping down the hill toward the tent, holding his arms above his head, trying to avert the rain. He runs a sharp turn around the clumsy newlyweds.

"Okay, let's just go on in the clubhouse and wait awhile," I suggest.

"No." Karen hands me her wine again and takes off after Anthony. I follow more slowly, trying not to spill the wine, covering it with my free hand.

Just as they reach the edge of the fluttering tent, Anthony stops and turns around. I catch up. Karen falls down. I don't see what she has tripped over, but I bend down and offer my free arm. Anthony is laughing.

"Are you hurt?" I ask her. She reaches for me, trying to untangle her shoulder strap from her ankle and arises slowly, but without dignity.

"Hey, goofnut, you tripped me!" She is glaring up at him.

"You don't need *my* help to make a fool of yourself," he smiles back.

She grabs her glass from me. And there it goes! An ordinary glass of thin, tinny red wine…right in Anthony's face, dripping over his round tortoise shelled eyeglasses, slithering off his chin. It becomes a purple rivulet, seeping and snuggling its way into the starched white folds of his tux shirt. "Come on, Karen," I say, pulling her toward the bar. "We need a refill."

Chewing Crystal

GOSSIP SOARS UP AND down Key West like lights on an electronic switchboard. So even though Gary orders the same '88 Australian shiraz we shared on the night we met, I am anxious.

Our waiter's blue nametag tells us his name is Rob. He is young, blonde. Bleached, I think, until I see the light, fine down on his darkly tanned forearms under the rolled-up sleeves of a starched white shirt.

Rob inserts the corkscrew and in one fluid motion slides out the cork. He places it ceremoniously on the table in front of Gary, who picks it up casually, sniffs it and nods. Rob fills my big round goblet. I taste it. Exotic spices, black pepper, and cherries toss their scents up my nose. Lush velvet slides down my throat. "Complex, yet balanced, soft, and dry … *Rob*," I say, then laugh at my own wit.

He ignores me, turns to Gary and fills his glass, then rewraps the Shiraz in a white linen napkin and parks it on the table between us. There it stands, like a little white-coated green soldier beside the center-piece, a small log of gray driftwood holding a fat white candle. A local artist, I am sure, has filled the driftwood's holes with silver bolts on which glass beads and baubles are suspended. They dance and jiggle in the candlelight, slinging shards of color across our table. "Twinkle, twinkle, baubles and beads," I say, gulping the shiraz.

Gary reaches into his inside blazer pocket, pulls out his tiny wire-rimmed reading glasses, places them on his nose and peeks at me over the top of them as he opens the large red leather menu. "What are you going to order?" he asks.

"Filet mignon," I answer. "More wine, please." I hold my empty glass aloft and see my frosty peach lipstick imprinted on its rim. Gary pours mine, then lifts his own glass slightly above his head and swirls it. I imagine it heaving itself right over onto the pris-tine tablecloth. Plop, Plop, the shiraz does a belly flop.

Rob returns, gets no further with the specials than "seared tuna" when Gary stops him. "Seared tuna for me, filet for my lady friend, house salads first." Rob eyes me curiously, pours more wine into my again empty glass.

"Seared tuna?" I laugh. "Can't you just see it? Charley and all his friends hovering over their camp-fire on the bottom of the ocean, roasting s'mores, their eyes neon green in the firelight, and suddenly poor, eager, hungry Charley gets too close and BINGO, seared tuna!" Gary stares at me. Rob giggles as he turns to leave. His luscious, round buttocks barely move under his tight black pants.

Silverware clinks, low rumblings of conversation and laughter increase in volume as bottles of the best vintages and frothy tropical drinks land on tables around us.

Our salads arrive, field greens, their sharp ruffled edges anointed with biting balsamic vinegar. I hold my glass up, smile for a refill, and Rob obliges, draining the last of the lovely Shiraz into my glass. "Thanks ... *Rob.*" I grin at him.

Tiny, navy blue Aztec warriors march dizzily around the edge of my salad plate as I try to swallow the bitter meadow greens. Gary's warriors are yellow. I stab at one of mine. It marches on. I look up at Gary as he chews quietly, his lips full and red from the wine, a perfect oval in the midst of his five o'clock shadow. I resist the urge to reach over and touch his face, to slide my fingertips in and out of his mouth, up and down his rough cheeks. Instead, I grip my wine goblet tightly.

Rob appears once more. He places our dinners in front of us, removes the frenzied warriors. My appetite is gone but would have left anyway when I looked at my steak. It is swimming in its own blood, which the garlic mashed potatoes have absorbed, sopping it up like gauze on an open wound.

I drink. Gary bites into his tuna, a bit of mango

salsa escapes his mouth and a dribble of orange shines on his chin in the candlelight. Before I can ponder it further, he wipes it away.

"How is cheered sarly?" I slur. "And while we're on the subject of dead fish, who is she?"

"Who is who?" he spears another bite, doesn't even look up.

"Don't play games with me. News travels like the speed of sound around here. I know there is someone else."

He sighs, puts down his fork, pushes away his plate and looks directly at me. Suddenly I want to bite into the crystal goblet, feel the crunch, the grinding of my teeth. Splinters will wedge between them and sparkle when I open my mouth. I will taste my own salty blood, I think, as it mingles with the tears that are already sliding into my mouth. They'll taste the same.

"Okay, time for honesty." His words jerk me back into reality, where I am greatly relieved to feel nothing in my mouth, except my teeth and tongue, which seem to be intact. No shards of chewed up glass poking around in my cheeks.

Gary signals for Rob, wipes his mouth, folds his napkin precisely, and places it beside his plate. I up-end my glass and pour the heavy remnants of the wine down my throat. Rob comes over, a small black tray with our bill in his hand. He sets it down, then leans over and whispers something into Gary's ear. His lips linger there. His tongue grazes Gary's earlobe. They are laughing.

"Meet 'someone else.'" Gary winks at me, rubbing his hand slowly over that cute taut butt.

Crayons in Heaven

"Why am i the only one that wears blue?" the little girl looked up at the large white- bearded man who pushed open the gate for her. It looked heavy. He was huffing with the effort, and his wireless glasses were misting over with perspiration. The gate joined an endless expanse of gold fencing with what seemed like hundreds of solemn-faced folks sitting atop it. They all wore white. The child looked down at her robe once more, just to be sure it was blue. It was. These people are all grown-ups, she thought, looking up and down the line of fencing on either side of the huge gate.

"I would like to see your children," she stated boldly to the man. He had opened the gate wide by then and beyond it a whole valley glittered intolerably, as white as pure snow. He sat down heavily next to her and produced a sparkling white handkerchief from an unseen pocket in his robe.

"One demand at a time, please," he looked at her kindly and mopped his brow. It was then that the little girl realized he was sitting on a cloud, she was standing on it, and the fence and all those serious people perched upon it were on the cloud, too. It was fluffy and white, of course, and she wondered how it was holding all of them up.

"I am Saint Latcher, keeper of the gate," the man peeked over his glasses at her.

"And I am Robin Egg, wearer of the blue robe," she mimicked him and doubled over with giggles. At that, all the people on the fence began laughing, too. It filled the glaring white space with a joyous roaring sound.

"No, I was only teasing, Mr. Latcher," her giggles subsided to a simple smile. "My name is Melissa. Where am I? Why am I the only child and why is my robe blue? The glare here hurts my eyes." Meanwhile, the folks on the fence grew quiet. Some were whispering among themselves, nodding and pointing at her.

"Who are those people? Please tell them it's not polite to point."

"Those people are hoping to become angels."

"Angels?" Melissa looked up and down the fence. "You mean they're on the fence waiting for their wings?" With that, the uproarious merriment began again. Some of them even fell off into the fluffiness of the cloud, and St. Latcher had to use his handkerchief once more to wipe his eyes, this time for tears of laughter.

Just then there came a fluttering sound and a whispering of wind.

"What in the name of heaven is going on out here?" An angel, or at least something human with beautiful soft feathery wings, was hovering over Melissa and St. Latcher. "God sent me out here to find out why everyone is laughing. We can't concentrate with all this noise."

A celestial hush fell. Melissa's eyes became huge. "No wonder everyone wants to be an angel," she said, looking up. "You are lovely. But how can you see? Flying around in all this dazzling whiteness?" The angel was, in fact, squinting.

"Well, now that you mention it, it is rather bright here," the angel told her. "I was just so happy to get my wings and become part of God's staff, I never thought about it."

"Oh, so now that you are an angel, you are part of his staff?" Melissa was amazed.

"Yes, that's how it works here. When we get our wings, we get to help him solve as many of the earthly problems as possible."

"Well, I would say God is understaffed," Melissa said sternly. "The problems on earth are serious. I mean there are lots of them, and they are really getting bad."

"Yes, I know, we can hear all the chaos down there."

"Hear it?? If it weren't so glary up here, you could

see it, too. And if you let all these people on the fence become angels right away, more problems could be solved. Many wings make light work," Melissa said. This time the folks on the fence clapped loudly.

And with that, the angel extended a hand. "Come on, young one, let's go talk to God."

When God saw Melissa's blue robe, he was puzzled. "How did you get into Heaven with a blue robe? And why aren't you in Children's Paradise with others your age?"

"I don't know, Sir," Melissa answered politely. "But here I am, and here is a box of colors." She reached into the pocket of her blue robe and handed Him a box of brand new Crayolas. "I think Heaven should be as colorful as earth. You could all see better up here. And…" she smiled up at God sweetly, "if everyone got their wings right away, problems might be solved on earth more quickly. No one likes being on the fence."

God looked down at Melissa, scratched His sacred chin and grinned. Then He laughed a loud and holy laugh that filled heaven. Clouds quivered, the golden fence shook, and although the folks on the fence tumbled off, they hit only air. They had wings.

And as they flew around, they were filled with awe and happiness at the sight of green valleys, blue skies, aqua seas, yellow flowers, and rainbows of all colors. Best of all were their robes. Each new angel sported a colored robe. Their wings, however, remained white.

Daisy

I WAS NOT BORN BLIND. I was sighted, in fact, for sixteen years, eight months, and five days—long enough to know that the world is filled with wonder—and long enough to take it all for granted. Most adolescents do.

We wake up to the light of day, see our faces in a mirror, shave without cutting ourselves; we know what is edible, see the world in a kaleidoscope of colors and changing textures, can find our abandoned mate to a running shoe while filling a backpack with each book the day's classes will require, and of course, drive a car—our first rite of passage into a mobile world.

Because I did see for a long time, I have a frame of reference. I guess you could say I am lucky. There are times I wonder how those who are born blind devise a context for their world. Maybe their devised reality is actually better than the one I know is out there. Maybe what they "see" is even more wondrous. I will never know.

What I do know is that when I was plunged into total darkness after the driver of an out of control car plunged through a red light, everything familiar became my enemy. Furniture lurked, hovered, and hid, waiting to throw itself against my leg or hip. Corridors, rooms, doors—all conspired to interrupt my awkward stumbling—to slap my face, pinch my groping hands. Foundations shifted, steps threw me hard against their comrades.

Blackness was not alone in tormenting me. Despair, isolation, anger, fear, helplessness all joined in consuming what was left of my sixteen-year life, which could accommodate none of it.

"Wake up! Today's the day!" I heard Frank, my roommate at Seeing Helpers School, before I felt his punch on my arm outside the covers. We had become friends during the twenty-six days we spent here, preparing for this very day.

I laughed. I had been awake for hours, eager and excited as a child on Christmas, a soon-to-be father in a waiting room.

Shouts of joy, water running, canes tap tapping in the hall, bits of conversation: "What if mine is goofy?" "Goofy is better than being in some sort of dog cult bent on self-sacrifice!" "I will teach mine to retrieve bikinis on the beach…"

We knew the physical world would not reappear. It will still jostle and overwhelm us, but now we would not be alone.

When my name was called, I tapped my way into the room where I would meet the helpmate who had been chosen just for me, matched in temperament, exposed to all social situations, displayed responsibility, dedication, a desire to please. How would the family who trained this exceptional animal handle the grief of losing it, I wondered.

Just then, Ann, my mobility trainer and now friend, sat me in a straight backed chair, placed her hands on my shoulders, and in a wavering voice full of emotion, said, "Your dog is a yellow lab, a female. Her name is Daisy. When we let her in, call her. And always use her name. She will be exuberant, so you can be silly for this encounter only." Ann removed her reassuring touch and stood aside. I heard the door open and my voice cracked, barely audible.

"Daisy, come," I managed to call, and the scrambling and snorting did not even register before she was upon me—paws on my shoulders, licking my face, kissing me, her tail batting my knees…Nothing in my training had prepared me for the sheer force of her—vigorous and powerful. We both tumbled to the floor, rolling, cuddling, laughing, and blathering. Ann laughed at her own trite joke, "Love at first sight."

We spent the next several weeks, Daisy and I, acquiring an array of mental and practical skills, and getting to know one another. We both learned that this job requires stamina and repetition—through the steel-handled leather harness she transmitted poise, confidence, reliability, and strength. I, the navigator, in turn relayed commands that I honed from a fine memory and spatial orientation—a parting gift to those who lose their sight later in life. Daisy's gift was the grace to know exactly when not to honor mine. I learned to not put her in a situation that would cause discomfort or double responsibility. My white cane is still my companion when visiting a zoo or rock concert. Large predatory animals and blaring speakers pose no threat to a stick.

〰

Today Daisy and I had lunch in our favorite deli down on 8th Avenue. We rode the bus. I am continually amazed how being blind heightens my senses to just how foolish the world's patterned responses to us really are. People call out to her, plop themselves into buildings to get out of our way, forget we can hear their comments, just to name a few. But on we go. I am upright and unafraid because she is brave and her judgment is always on target. There is not one thing patronizing or sentimental about her job—until she is out of her harness. Then she becomes my friend, playmate, ball retriever, and listener.

"What do you think, Miss Daisy?" I will say to her. "A short trek today or a long one? How about ice cream after that long art history class? Or maybe we will be good and do lunch?" She brings me her harness, heads for the door and thumps her tail as she waits for me to put it on her.

Many times I miscalculate, am unaware. She pushed herself in front of me, hard, yesterday at a curb right before a fast-moving cab jumped it, and left a fender and a spinning tire directly in our hastily-abandoned path. People beside us "oohed" and "aahed." "Good girl, Daisy. Thank you." I rubbed her soft forehead, tickled her ears, and felt her smile up at me.

Ghostnannies

JEREMY BROWN AND HIS twin sister, Jenny, were
sent to bed early on moving day. Their parents were
cranky with everyone, even Buster, the six month old
black lab.

Buster had run away twice. He burrowed his wiggly, energetic body through a small opening in the
backyard fence. He jumped on a moving man, bouncing him down the stairs on his bottom. An antique
chest the man insisted he could carry alone bobbed
along with him. Drawers flew everywhere. His yelling, Buster's barking, and the twins' hysteria made
screeching harmony, accompanied by the cracking
of breaking wood.

Mrs. Brown's favorite Italian platter arrived in
pieces. The TV cable man never showed up. The
family's dinner pizza was delivered cold and soggy

because Mr. Brown had accidentally given Domino's their old address. Mounds of white crinkled packing paper littered the downstairs.

Upstairs the twins were whining about having to sleep in the same room.

"The other bedroom must be repainted," their mother sighed, while rooting around in their matching suitcases for toothbrushes. Mr. Brown was trying to put sheets on the single beds. "We had to wait a long time for this house to become available."

"Yeah, we had to wait for old Mrs. Allen to die and move on to ghostland." Jeremy fell back onto his bed, laughing and rolling around, instantly untucking the sheets. Jenny giggled and climbed into the other single bed.

Both parents frowned. "I can't find the toothbrushes. Just go to sleep," their mother said and kissed them goodnight.

The twins were still giggling when an old woman oozed out of the bedroom closet and floated over to the window seat. She sat down and produced a ball of white yarn and two silver knitting needles. She looked cloudy, but Jeremy and Jenny could see the trees outside the window right through her. She smelled like flowers and baby powder.

"It's a ghost!" shrieked Jenny, sitting straight up. Jeremy stuffed his fist into his mouth and jumped into Jenny's bed.

"Yes, I am Mrs. Allen." She began clicking and clacking her needles up and down as the yarn unraveled. Both children leaped for the door.

"Oh, don't bother calling your parents. They won't believe you, and they certainly can't see me. I am a children's ghost. You see, I always wanted children, and now I have you two. I actually thought the Good Lord would let me be a guardian angel, but it seems there was a waiting list, so here I am! Not my first choice, but He works in mysterious ways so I know it will work out well."

The twins stared at her. "Just call me Ghostnanny," she smiled at them. "Now go to sleep. We'll begin our fun tomorrow."

Jeremy and Jenny climbed back into their beds and fell into an exhausted sleep to the rhythm of clicking and clacking.

The next night, another ghost appeared. He pulled Jeremy's desk chair over to the window beside Mrs. Allen. He unfolded an old yellow newspaper, began moving his head back and forth, and crunching small, hard, butterscotch candies that he pulled from an unseen pocket. He chattered so incessantly that Mrs. Allen finally smacked the newspaper with her knitting needles. "Hush," she told him. He didn't.

Another ghostnanny appeared each night. By the fourth night, the twins were tired. Their evenings were filled with endless chatter, clicking needles, toe tickling, giggling, newspaper rattling, hymn singing, calypso dancing and storytelling.

On Saturday morning they sat bleary eyed in their new tree house. Jeremy hugged his knees. Jenny squinted up at the sky. "Five ghostnannies are just too many," she said. "I have a plan."

That night the twins convinced the ghostnannies to go with them for a walk. They stumbled down the street. The noisy ghosts floated along behind them. At the end of the cul-de-sac, Jenny and Jeremy led them across an unkempt lawn scattered with toy trucks, tricycles, plastic logs, shovels and pails. An empty sandbox sat atop a pile of sand. They peeked in the living room window.

Inside were five small children. One was sitting in a wind-up swing that had stopped swinging. He was wailing loudly. Two were crawling along the floor. One of them stopped to smear the gooey remains of an animal cracker across the screen of a large TV where Dora the Explorer was peeking through binoculars.

The other crawler pulled herself up on a coffee table heaped with magazines. She threw them across the room one by one, squealing loudly as each one hit the floor, then looked down, untaped her diaper and hurled that, too. Another child, about four, held in a headlock by his older sister, screamed something inaudible while trying to kick her legs out from under her.

Their mother sat unmoving and expressionless on the sofa. It was hard to tell her apart from the row of stuffed animals lined up beside her.

Outside, Jenny turned to the ghostnannies. "Just think," she said. "They aren't even in school yet so you guys could enjoy entertaining them all day. You could rotate kids." Mrs. Allen scratched her cloudy chin. "That would be rather nice. One on one attention is endorsed by experts." The ghostnannies looked at one another, nodded and began clapping.

They bid the twins farewell, promised to visit, and disappeared in a line through the front door, chattering, singing, and dancing.

The tired mother never knew why her children became so tranquil and content. She didn't care either.

Foothills

I HEAR THE COPPERHEADS SLITHERING around in the small, meshed, locked cage under my stiff single bed, the one donated to us by the ladies of Mt. Stone Holy Redeemer Tabernacle. They actually gave us two, and my sister Naomi sleeps in the other one right across from me. The rattlers are under hers.

We don't mind though, we've been bedding down over these cages since we left the crib. If people at church ask Daddy where he keeps his snakes, he laughs and says, "Why right in the house with us, of course," not letting on just where in the house they stay. I never have friends over to visit or spend the night, so I don't have to watch them stare under our beds, listen to them scream, or answer their endless silly questions.

Anyway, tonight the moon is full, and I watch it

through our bedroom window. Naomi is sleeping so quietly, I really have time to think. She's younger than me, only eight, and doesn't have things she has to mull over yet, like I do because I'm thirteen.

What I'm pondering tonight, while that big old shining moon throws light on me, is how I can help Daddy catch his snakes. It's getting harder to keep as many as he needs. When they get too feisty we have to let them go, and it seems like lately they get testy sooner that they used to.

He takes me with him up to the foothills around our house below the Unaka Mountains where the pine trees are so tall I can't see the tops of them, and the ground is covered with their needles and rocks of all shapes and sizes, mostly gray. He lumbers ahead of me, supporting himself on that long, forked oak stick he carries because the path is shifty with those loose stones.

He tells me his secrets. "Yep, Pauline, there's no better way to bring folks to the Lord. Praising His holy name and shouting with joy while handling those poisonous serpents is the best way to teach them. It makes evil real to them. They can see right before their very eyes that Satan can be overcome!" He sure does get excited.

I am named after the apostle Paul, writer of several Bible books, Romans being my favorite, and I don't doubt for a minute the power Daddy holds over his congregation by handling those snakes. I've seen folks fall on their knees, eyes closed, fists clenched, moaning like mortal pain will soon sweep them away, only to jump up again, clap their hands over their heads and scream "Hallelujah! You've shown us His power, Preacher!" or something along those lines.

One time Mrs. Taylor fainted dead away, and Daddy quickly handed the big ol' slinky copperhead to Deacon John, who was standing beside him, and ran over and put his rough, scarred hand right on her sweaty forehead. He healed her on the spot! She sat up then, tears sliding down her face, and whispered, "You done it, Preacher. Drove the devil right outta me. Praise God."

Meanwhile, Deacon John, who never touches the serpents, is just there to help rile up the congregation, howled and blubbered. We thought he was speaking in tongues but turned out he was screaming in mortal terror. He dropped that creature so fast you'd a thought it bit his hand or had skin hot enough to burn through his fingers. It slithered behind the pulpit and coiled itself up.

Daddy said the benediction real fast then and people ran on out the front door. I just about wet my pants, trying to keep from laughing. "No place for levity in the house of God, Pauline," Daddy said when he saw me dancin' around.

No, I don't doubt the clout of Daddy or those snakes for a minute. I do, though, believe I have a better way to catch them. Like I told you, we tromp through the hills, him sharing his thoughts and all, and I hear the tiredness in his voice. You see, his breath doesn't get to him fast as it used to. His face gets red, and he stumbles a lot.

To tell the truth, I'm afraid he'll tumble right over, gasping for air and I won't get down the hills fast enough to get Mama. She couldn't get up to us anyway. She's never been one to move too fast. Sometimes I see her from far up, hanging Daddy's white shirts on the line, and she'll wave up to us, but I know she'd never hear me shouting for help.

And one of these days when he leans over to roll one of them weighty rocks away to look underneath it, he just might lose his balance. Then that big forked stick will fly outta his hand and well…. you get the picture. I don't think Jesus himself could keep a snake from striking with all that chaos, the ground shaking and quaking while Daddy tries to stand up without his cane.

So, now I think I came up with a better way. I know snakes pretty well. What they like are soft things and slithering up trees, though Daddy never figured out how to get the ones lying around up there. I'll get some of Mama's old nylon stockings, ones she can't wear anymore because her garter caught them under the rims and tore holes that sent runners all the way to the toes. I'll fill them with lint from our old Sears Roebuck washer after I've laid it out in the sun to dry. Then I'll climb up every oak, maple, and gum tree along our favorite paths, nail them tight, open end up, on the branches. Once those snakes slide up the tree and into those old stockings stuffed with soft fluffy lint, they are caught! They'll glide right down and settle in and won't be able to wiggle out at all. I'll keep this up until our cages are brimming over. Daddy and I will haul them in the back of the pickup right over to the Mt. Stone Holy Redeemer Tabernacle. Then he can brag to all his church folks that his very own daughter, Miss Pauline Harmon, caught them herself. Praise the Lord!

Divine Decisions

Aɴᴅ ꜱᴏ ɪᴛ ᴄᴀᴍᴇ to pass that in the year 2010, God chose Fairchild and Goodfellow, two of the angels on His staff, to be His advisors for that year. Being God's yearly advisor was, indeed, a special privilege. They were allowed to sit on God's shoulders and help Him make decisions for His questionable creation—mankind. God was wise, of course, always choosing angels with differing opinions. He liked to hear both sides before deciding anything.

God knew that Fairchild and Goodfellow were opposites, but it was October and He was getting a little weary with just how contrary to one another they were. They bickered a little more than He liked, so He had taken to rocking in His huge gold rocking chair while they sat and argued on his shoulders— one on each. It soothed God and often rocked them both to sleep—an interval of divine relief. All of heaven loved it when God rocked. The gentle back and forth motion provided a blissful, celestial squeak and a soft, rapturous wind.

Now Goodfellow and Fairchild, although argumentative, really did deserve the honor. They were loyal and faithful. Many angels, as some earthlings realize, soar back and forth to earth when something exceptionally humorous or tragic occurs (which is constantly) to be entertained or offer assistance. Sometimes they just hover around down there, forgetting to come back to Heaven. They really can be flighty.

Today, however, Fairchild and Goodfellow were lulled into neither contemplation nor sleep while God was rocking.

"The Middle East is a mess! I believe You should destroy the earth and start over. I know creation is hard work but You did it before, and now you have Your staff to help," Goodfellow bellowed.

"Are you crazy?" Fairchild asked reverently. He always remained reverent in God's presence, even when trying to make a point. "Mankind deserves a chance to right itself. Those silly humans are human, after all, and they will suffer their own consequences, and then get it right."

God said nothing so Goodfellow continued his argument. "No, the time is now! You predicted this mess ending when war became prevalent in Your Son's homeland. Revelation says so!"

"Revelation, my fellow advisor and good friend,

is only the loosely written ramblings of a hallucinating man during imprisonment. Anyway, it is only an allegory, isn't it, God?" Fairchild calmly said.

Not moving His head, God rolled His eyes left and right, looking first at one and then the other. Next He rolled His eyes heavenward (or up from there).

"Allegory, smallegory!" Now Goodfellow's voice was rising even more. "They're destroying the earth You created for them, as well as each other. Disease is rampant, suffering is at an all-time high, not to mention greed, avarice, lust, revenge, murder....

I say 'go for it', God. We will help You with the next batch."

"Yes, you are quite right, Goodfellow," said Fairchild, "But consider all that is good about mankind. Many of them really do make an effort to pray, worship, follow the rules, and be kind, loving and careful. I believe they will all come around eventually. Let's give them another chance."

Just then there came a flapping of hot air and a stale odor—a blur of red. Satan himself flitted up and plopped down on God's lap. God's brow furrowed. His eyes narrowed. He looked angrily at Satan.

"Neither of you is right, you half-witted seraphic advisors. I will attain full power over man. I have made great headway already," Satan laughed wickedly. "It's just a matter of time. I will destroy them myself with internal agitation until they all murder one another." His grin was evil.

God spoke. "Yes, Luce, my old arch enemy, you have won battles, but I will win the war. In fact, I've

already put my Son, J.C., on it. Remember Him?"
His brow softened at the thought of His Son.

"Hellfire and damnation!" Satan bellowed. "Of
course I remember Him. I chatted with Him a few
times—'get thee behind me' and all that stuff. He
is one hell of a powerful general. I just love to stir
up trouble and besides, I was hoping You had fired
Him by now. I had to try again." He choked in a fit
of coughing. "Hell, the air is too pure up here." He
pulled himself up, balancing one foot on each of
God's knees, fluttered his red cape and flew off.

God started laughing, and the heavens shook merrily. Fairchild and Goodfellow almost fell off His
shoulders. They each grabbed an ear for balance.
His laughter finally subsided, and Goodfellow and
Fairchild regained their balance. All three continued
to rock—peaceful and deep in hallowed thought.

Halloween Dinner

Abigail's yellow eyes sparkled as she skipped along the leaf-encrusted path that led to the back door of her stone cottage. It was twilight. She had been out in the woods completing her evening chores and thinking happily of her family's traditional Halloween dinner. She ignored the thorny bushes that grew tall and doubled over on either side of the path. Holding tightly to her woven basket, she pushed open the heavy wooden door, then slammed it behind her, harder than she intended.

"Ouch!" the door frame hollered. "Easy, kid."

"Oops, sorry," she apologized and walked into the kitchen where her mother was chopping insects on the cement countertop. Two huge furry rats sat on tall brown toadstools at the end of the counter watching the paper thin wings and legs scatter. They covered their ears with their paws each time the razor-sharp ax came down with a thud.

Abigail plopped the basket down near the rats and climbed up beside them.

"So, how many did you find?" her mother smiled at her.

"Ten," she answered, lifting off the lid. Ten large hairy spiders were scurrying around inside. Abigail reached in and pulled one out. It fell to the floor and hurried away.

"Well, now you only have nine," one of the rats laughed.

"Hand me the basket, please," her mother said. "I need to get these spiders marinated. Our guests will be arriving soon."

"Yum, yum, marinated spiders," the other rat rubbed his furry fat tummy.

Her mother poured the spiders into a bowl and covered them with a syrupy green liquid that smelled like wet grass. "Abigail, please set the table."

She did. Her mother scraped the remaining insect parts into a huge black iron pot overhanging the fire in the rock fireplace. It sizzled and crackled.

"Bug stew, I hope?" Abigail asked.

"Yes, your favorite. It should be especially good tonight. Roaches and centipedes are abundant in autumn."

Suddenly, they heard scratching and yowling at the kitchen window. Fiery red eyes peered in at them. Sharp toenails scraped against the glass.

"Oh, no, did you forget to feed the vampire wolves?" Abigail's mother looked at her.

"Oops, I did forget," Abigail said. She skipped over to the black steel refrigerated coffin, opened the door and peered in. "Mom, we are out of blood."

"I guess we are both forgetful today. Could you please fly over to the 12-12 and pick up a gallon? We can't have the pets creating bedlam out there during dinner."

Abigail ran outside and grabbed her broom. The moon was winking merrily in the sky.

"Where are we going?" her broom asked, as she climbed aboard and soared upward.

"To the 12-12," Abigail answered. "Mom forgot to get blood today, and the wolves are going crazy."

"I heard the ruckus," the broom laughed. "Watch out. Remember what night it is."

Broom traffic was always heavy on Halloween. Abigail was glad the moon was full. She landed and propped her broom outside the store. A black cat perched on the checkout counter meowed loudly when she opened the door.

"Well, Miss Abby, what did your mother forget?" Franklin Stein, the store manager, teased her when she walked in.

"Blood for the vampire wolves," Abigail smiled and retrieved a gallon container from the refrigerated glass caskets at the back of the store.

"Pay me next time," Mr. Stein told her. "Happy Halloween."

"Thank you. We are having special dinner guests."

She flew home, scampered into the backyard and poured the blood into a huge gray kettle. Frenzied and greedy, the wolves streamed at her from all directions, baring their luminous green teeth.

"Sit!" she admonished sternly. They did, all at once, looking up at her shyly. "I know you are hungry, but where are your manners?" She shook her finger at them and ran into the house.

Bleached skulls, bone spoons and forks gleamed in the candlelight, simmering bug stew gurgled in the pot and marinated spider parts filled a large hollow pumpkin in the middle of the table. Her mother had even convinced the bats to hold the place cards. Their red beady eyes looked around upside down. Then she saw the dinner guests.

"Aunt Mummy and Uncle Monster!" Abigail shouted and ran to them for a hug. "I hope you brought lizard gizzard pudding for dessert!" Her aunt nodded and both of them hugged her tightly.

The two rats were already sitting on toadstools at the table. They had snakeskin napkins tied under their chins and were holding their bone forks aloft.

"You guys are as unmannerly as the wolves," Abigail laughed.

"Hurry and sit down," one of them winked. "We're hungry."

Hi Ho Silver

THE DOORS OPEN AUTOMATICALLY for me—inward, of course. A huge vase of plastic flowers on a round pedestal table greet me. Paisley on the wall-to-wall carpet matches the bouquet, pinks and greens swirling and dancing, a dizzying stage for the lifeless flowers.

Strong disinfectant, old urine, and cloying air freshener weave up my nose and I squint into the dimness. Outside the sun is shining hotly and brightly. I wonder how those old people sitting on the wooden benches on either side of the glass doors that swing inward can smoke in the heat. They sit, their canes and walkers propped beside their wasting bodies, puffing and blowing.

An array of strong-looking women in light blue uniforms sits with them, sucking on Newports and laughing among themselves. I feel sure they are glad for the break outside, the rush of each puff a relief from wiping sagging old fannies and enduring endless nonsensical jabber or stony silence from those they serve.

The elderly smokers inhale and exhale, a rhythm filling a need too desperate to be abandoned, too long a part of them to worry about, too much a change of routine—an escape from the grim reality of being herded like a cow through a meaningless day. Something to live for.

My mother-in-law used to smoke, too. She'd be sitting out there with them now, enjoying her "ciggie" if she hadn't forgotten that she smoked. The doors whish closed behind me. I continue to the elevator and press two, grateful to find it empty when it lands.

I get off on two, walk by the beauty parlor where a middle-aged, pink-smocked lady with frizzy gray hair is laughing gaily while her client snores loudly, her mouth empty and hanging open, her head bent back over the sink.

"Hey, Rita." I peek my head through the door.

"Hey yourself, girlfriend. How ya doin'? Check out your mother-in-law's manicure today. Pretty new colors, she chose a different one for each nail."

"Yep, that sounds just like her. Purple and pink are her favorites. She hates dark colors, always told us they reminded her of death. At least her sense of color is still intact. Anyway, thank you for keeping her so nicely groomed." I mean it, too. What a job, rubbing all that flaky, thin-haired scalp and painting old brittle nails.

"My pleasure. And don't kid yourself. Her sense of humor is still there, too. She's a sweet old thing."

"Thank you, God, for all the Ritas in the world," I say silently.

Several attendants sit at the nurse's station. Their heads are bent over stacks of paper. They ignore me as I turn right down the hall to Room 214, where my stomach lurches as I peek in the door. I never know what I'll find.

As usual, my mother-in-law is sitting in her wheelchair staring out the window. The blooming violet I brought her last week has wilted on the windowsill. Her room is cluttered—old family pictures, random large print Reader's Digests, unopened Valentine candy, a waterless vase of dead flowers, their bare stems brown and sagging, and cards from grandchildren, lined up and signed with scraggly names the parents tried to make look authentic.

"Hi, Dottie," I say loudly, cheerfully. She turns around, smiles a toothless smile.

"Oh, hello dear, how are you?"

"I'm fine, Dottie, why don't you have your teeth in?"

"What?" she continues to smile up at me. I approach her and turn her chair away from the window, sit down on her bed, facing her.

"Your teeth, Dottie, where are your teeth?"

"Oh, they're out in the car, driving around."

"Okay." I make a mental note to ask the nurses about them when I leave.

"You're looking well. Just look at your nails." I

take her hands in mine. "Rita told me you picked all these lovely colors. Don't they look great?"

She looks at her nails. "Oh, yes, Sybil did them for me." Sybil was her grandmother's name. "I'm going home tomorrow."

"You are? Well, that's good." I get up and walk to her closet. Sure enough, her open suitcase is on the floor—underwear, stockings, and slips spilling over the edges, one lavender Ked sitting atop the clutter. "I see you're packed." I turn back to her.

Just then a long, low moan winds its way down the hall. I look out the door. There on the paisley carpet a woman, naked from the waist up, has propped her upper body on her elbows, her legs still and useless, her overturned wheelchair just inches behind her.

Her breasts are perfectly rounded, her skin flaw-less, milky. She continues moaning. I pick up her wheelchair and look right into her face. "Are you okay?"

She says nothing, stares at me blankly.

"She doesn't talk," my mother-in-law hollers be-hind me. "But she's always falling off her damned horse. Thing is too plucky to hold onto."

I step carefully over her and run to the nurse's station.

"That woman has fallen from her chair," I say loudly, pointing down the hall. The two attendants do not look up. I raise my voice to the tops of their bent heads. "Can't we get her back in her chair? And put some clothes on her?"

"She always falls off her horse when she's in her

underwear. I think it is slippery. Or maybe the saddle is just slick," one of them mutters and continues writing on a clipboard.

That night I dream I am waiting in the carpool line for my daughter to finish hockey practice. Moms sit in cars in front of and behind me. I look down and realize I am naked on a huge brown leather saddle. A long mane of stiff horse hair is swinging back and forth as the animal shakes its head and paws at the pavement.

Secrets

I SAW THEM KISSING IN the tree house next door. Mr. Baker had built a sturdy one for his ever expanding brood of noisy, Catholic children—plain and strong like the ancient oak to which it was nailed. Fluttering leaves and shards of sunlight did not hide their lust, their gentle groping. It disgusted me, or so I thought, but I couldn't look away. My juices churned right along with my stomach.

Just then my mother opened the back door, "Connie, find Hopper and tell him dinner is ready." I jumped, turned around and looked directly in her face, hoping to distract her. I shouldn't have worried; she was gazing at the melting ice in her glass, her eyes dull and glazed over, "Damn, I need another drink." She returned to the kitchen. I called to Hopper.

We were both flushed at dinner that night, Hopper and I, squirming in our chairs, peering at each other over our glass rims. He knew I had seen him. I knew an unspoken truth would rest peacefully between us. I think it was the only secret he and I never talked about. When Margaret or Mary joked about queers and displayed limp wrists, they looked directly at him and laughed.

"No son of mine is light on his feet!" my father would shout at dinner, then slap the table and sometimes Hopper, hard for emphasis. Mother never said anything. She smoked and drank her dinner, then stumbled upstairs mumbling, "Do the dishes, kids, and don't forget to wipe the countertops. Put the placemats in the washer."

I heard Margaret retching through the wall. "One, two, three…" I began counting to myself, wondering how long it would take her this time. She fumbled at my door, "Help me, Connie, I don't feel so well." I turned on my lamp, tiptoed across the room, and opened the door. She was propped against the doorframe and grabbed my arm. Her weight almost pulled me over. I guided her back to her bed. She fell heavily. I tucked her comforter up around her and returned to the bathroom for a cold cloth and aspirin.

"This Nurse Nancy routine is wearing me down. God, I look tired," I spoke aloud to pale, heavy-lidded, person looking at me from inside the harshly lit mirror. By the time I had returned, she was asleep.

I put the cold cloth on her forehead anyway, then reached under her bed and pulled out the empty vodka bottle.

Margaret was not at breakfast the next day. "I thought I heard her up in the night," Mother said. "Did you hear her, Connie? Go check on her and see if she's feeling unwell. Maybe she needs a Midol." She rummaged through the vitamin drawer.

"What she needs is AA."

"Oh my," my mother murmured.

"AA is for derelicts and drunks!" Father shouted, shaking his fist in my face. I retreated upstairs.

〜

I pulled Mary through the noisy crowd of demonstrators. Most of them were hurling angry words and holding hastily drawn signs above their heads. We jostled and shoved our way up to the clinic door, slamming it quickly behind us. The room was hushed; stony women buried their heads in ratty magazines. We found an old green upholstered sofa and sat down.

"You'd better register with the receptionist," I told her, noticing the very young couple sitting across from us. "Cheryl Cheerleader and Fred Football Star," I whispered, but Mary didn't hear me. She had gotten up.

"Is it true there are garbage cans out back full of tiny torn body parts? If it is, I can't do this," the cheerleader-type girl began sobbing softly, burying her head in his football jacket. He looked at me helplessly. I wanted to nod yes, but shook my head back and forth. "No, no, not at all," he stroked her head.

I watched my sister register, tried to imagine her guilt as a snake, slithering its way through the labyrinth of her Catholic brain. "No amount of crying and begging for forgiveness behind the curtains of our confessional will erase this one," I said to myself. "The truth will always be in you."

Ironic, isn't it, a religion that instills guilt is haughty enough to teach that only a priest can absolve it? Father Frank's truth is as veiled as the cubicle he sits in, dispensing his conditions for forgiveness.

They were all young, I think. At least the one I saw looked about eighteen. She reminded me of a doe caught in headlights, peeking out from under my mother's 500 thread-count cotton sheets. My father's large white hairless bottom was still hovering over her—he obviously wasn't as quick or agile as his prey. I backed out quickly and ran down the hall. He was on my heels, trying to tie the belt of his navy blue silk bathrobe.

"Constance, why in the hell are you home from school this time of day?"

I saw Hopper today, quite by accident. Or more accurately, by a touch of grace. He was standing at the gate of St. Ann's Convent, where I was on my way downstairs and happened to glance out the stairway window. I knew he was thinking about me. We both knew he would not be allowed to enter.

"You are so dear to me," I said to him, pressing my face into the window. "I pray for you every day, for serenity and happiness in your life—in Margaret and Mary's, too." I turned away, thanking God that our theology did not destroy my faith. Silent confinement comes easily for me. I am well trained.

Moonwalk

NED EVANS AND BEN Austin had just flown through the moon's shadow. They were still thousands of miles away from the moon, but close enough that it filled the entire circular window of Apollo 11. It was eclipsing the sun at that moment, illuminated only by blue-gray earthshine and offering a dramatic and astonishing three-dimensional sight. Both astronauts were momentarily silenced by awe. Or perhaps fear. They returned to their work.

"What metaphor will earthlings use now for the unattainable?" Ned laughed.

"You mean like 'Hey, man, you could no more do that than fly to the moon?'" Ben asked. "Who knows, I am sure someone will come up with something. What I really want to know is what you are going to say into that mike when you make the first step."

"I have been bombarded with suggestions for months, everything from whole scenes of Shakespeare to lengthy Bible passages. I honestly don't know. Maybe something simple I heard my fifth grade teacher say when I first studied the moon," Ned said.

"How about, 'Here we are hammering our American flag and leaving a plaque saying we come to the moon in peace for all mankind.' Oh, and by the way, our country is dropping bombs in Southeast Asia. Let's congratulate ourselves for our humanity," Austin said.

"Yeah, too bad whoever landed on the earth first didn't make peace a prerequisite for residence," Ned added. They chuckled.

Hours later the lunar module Eagle touched down on the moon. It sank only a little, and speculations that the moon's surface might be overlaid with a thick coating of dust were put to rest. Visions of the Eagle and its occupants disappearing into a huge whole had troubled many. A collective sigh of relief went up around the world.

Austin and Evans suited up with pressure suits, gloves, helmets, portable oxygen supplies, life support systems, remote control units, water pumps and oxygen fan switches, and a mount for the lunar surface camera. Evans descended first. Before he pulled the ring to turn on the television camera, he looked up at his partner.

"Don't lock us out, buddy."

Austin smiled down at him, gave him a thumbs up

and answered, "I won't. Don't tear your suit on that
ladder, man. You just might ooze away."

And as Evans set foot on the crunchy, ancient gray
lava, he made his famous remark to a waiting earth.
"That's one small step for man, one giant leap for
mankind." Both men then began that odd bounding
motion now known as "moonwalking."

My brother Tommy and I sat cross legged on our
Aunt Edith's faded shag rug in front of her new RCA
color TV that hot July night. Our yearly stay with
her on her rural farm in southern Ohio overlapped
the historic event. Tommy was ten. I had just turned
twelve.

Aunt Edith had just put a pan of homemade brownies in the oven to celebrate. A rich chocolate aroma
began overtaking the smell of the fried chicken we
devoured at dinner. We sat still, glued to a picture on
the screen we had only seen in our rocket books.

The night was taking on an air of intense excite-
ment, not just because the media had overwhelmed
the nation with anticipation and concern, but more
importantly, because Aunt Edith had been Mr. Ned
Evan's fifth grade teacher. Tending the farm took her
right out of her classroom at Wapakoneta Elementary
School after our Uncle Stanford died unexpectedly.
She never complained, though the only children she
would ever have were her students.

"Yep," she had said about a hundred times since we arrived. "I am the one who taught that boy all about flying and space. I knew when he made the best solar system in the class that he would do something famous someday. We used starch and yarn to wrap balloons, you know. Then when the yarn dried, we popped the balloons and bingo! Solar systems!"

She yelled because she was hard of hearing, then slapped her knee, and continued rocking wildly in her rocking chair, giving us a glimpse of her rolled up nylon stockings when her feet lifted up on the backswing. She had taken off her old lady black lace-up shoes and placed them on the floor next to her chair. We nodded and smiled up at her, too respectful to remind her that she had confirmed this information many times already. Besides, the TV was at full volume.

"You boys will be walking on the moon yourselves one day, thanks to Mr. Ned Evans and me. He talked a lot about it, yes he did. And I told him, 'a man must be ever mindful of the steps he takes, in case they become leaps for another person.'"

I was picturing myself trying to walk on the moon with all that gear when Tommy turned around and bellowed, "You are probably right, Auntie, but walking on the moon won't be half as much fun as riding in your hay wagon!"

She laughed and leaned so far back I was afraid the chair would tip completely over. Her legs pointed heavenward that time.

Aunt Edith never skipped an evening hitching

up her old green John Deere to the rattly, wooden-planked hay wagon and hauling us along, bouncing and clapping behind her, while she made a last check of her livestock. "My kiddos," she called her pigs and cows. Her wide-brimmed straw hat that tied under her chin had always fallen off by then, and it hung down between her shoulders, exposing a tight steel-gray bun pinned up on the back of her head.

Farm hands came and went during those years, but Aunt Edith always made the last good night to her "kiddos" herself. I envied them being in her full-time care.

As Ned Evans took man's first step onto the surface of the moon and made his famous remark, Aunt Edith's eyes grew large and round.

"Well, I'll be! Did you hear that? We BOTH made history tonight!" And we all jumped up, held hands and danced in a circle, whooping and hollering until the brownies were done.

Life Lessons

A LARGE PURPLE BUS STOPS at the curb in front of us. We are expecting it. The yellow letters on the side say "TAG." We know that usually means "talented and gifted," but in this case, it means "tedious and grave."

About twenty young teenagers disembark when the big bus doors swish open. They line up along the sidewalk and look around, absorbing their surroundings like a complicated equation—eyes somber and squinting.

Anyone passing on the street would just see a group of youngsters, all shapes and sizes, some in jeans, some in skirts, some frizzy heads, some long, shiny-haired model types, and some in baggy pants and baseball caps turned backwards.

We hold the door open and in they go, one by one,

as if the building is sucking them in. "Welcome to
Real Life Day School," we say. "We will be your
escorts today. If you have questions, forget them. We
don't care what you think or why you think it."

The front hallway is dark and we lead them to
its end, where a huge wooden door holds a plaque
which reads, "Life Movement."

We all file in. Surround sound fills our ears with
Motown. A woman is on stage. She resembles Patti
LaBelle. Dressed in a tight, red dress and spiked
red high heels, she cracks a long, black whip. She
snaps it on the stage floor and points to an empty
screen that pops up behind her. "Here's your Life
Movement lesson for today!" she bellows out at us.
"It doesn't matter how you dance, just dance!" and
the big screen begins blinking with neon lights as
the Temptations come into view. Some of the teenagers hold their ears and back away. The whip cracks
once more. They move back to the group and "Patti"
shouts, "Watch me!" We all start to shag. The students do not take their eyes off her while they try to
follow her steps.

"Heard It Through the Grapevine" gives way
to Fleetwood Mac and on we go. The Beach Boys
"Catch a Wave," and before long, the young ones are
shagging pretty well.

Next we move on to Disco. The Bee Gees blare
through the surround sound. They are "Stayin' Alive"
while John Travolta wiggles his hips and struts his
stuff up on the lighted screen.

Kevin Bacon begins to "Cut Loose" and the crowd

attempts the complicated footwork. Cowboys and their ladies fill the screen with Stetsons and clicking Tony Llamas while they do the "Boot Scootin' Boogy" around and around. We end the hour hip-hopping to Eminem and Ice Ice Baby. The youngsters are sweating and clapping now. The lights come up and we all shout, "More! More!"

Patti cracks her whip again and shouts, "Okay, one more. You can never dance too much in life." And we calypso our way right out of "Life Movement" to Bob Marley's steel drum rendition of "Three Little Birds ... On My Doorstep ... Don't Worry, Be Happy."

It's on to "Life Economics." We all take seats in rows of folding chairs facing a stage upon which a dignified gentleman in a tweed jacket and burgundy bow tie stands regally behind a lectern. The kids are still breathing heavily but smiling.

The gentleman raps a gavel, peers out at us over a small, thin pair of wire glasses and says seriously, "You get fined when you do wrong. You get taxed when you do right. Go figure. Remember that, despite the cost of living, it the always the best choice." He smiles then and nods, and we head around the corner to our next class, "Life Driving."

Once again, we sit facing a stage. A man is pacing back and forth on it. He is huge and muscled. He wears tight jeans tucked neatly into leather biking boots and a silver studded vest with nothing on beneath it except an impressive assortment of intricate tattoos. His gray hair is pulled back into a pony tail.

He taps gently at each point of his driving lesson, which is written out in elegant script on the blackboard behind him. His voice is a lullaby:

Be sure your horn does not get stuck when following a pack of Hell's Angels on the highway.

If you lined up all the cars in the United States end to end, one person would be stupid enough to try and pass them all. Do not be that person.

And if you decide beauty is in the eye of the beer holder, do not drive.

Lead belongs in your pencil, not in your shoes.

When it is your turn to be the designated driver, drop everyone off at the wrong house.

Mr. Muscle smiles and bows gracefully. We cheer and stomp our feet.

Our final class for today is "Life Philosophy." Here, sitting on a stage, are a priest, a minister, and a regular, but greasy looking guy in a lime green, polyester jacket with gelled hair. The priest stands up first. "Never trust a celibate man in a robe." He swishes his own for emphasis. "Oh, and remember," he continues, "You can talk to Jesus without asking His mother first."

Next the greasy looking guy stands up and waves his Bible around in the air.

"Praise the Lord, brothers and sisters! I say repent and be saved! I also say there is a fine line between revival preaching and mental illness!" He yells and we all hoot and holler. He does sort of a jumping body shake, spins completely around, and sits back down.

The minister stands up. His clerical collar makes his Adam's apple looked cramped. He smiles, tells us to write this down, and holds out his arms. We listen benevolently and write:

"Forgive everyone. It allows God to stay in charge. We don't want that job, anyway. The light at the end of the tunnel is usually an oncoming train so....make your own light. Live and love avidly. Enrich others and remember to enrich yourself, too. Celebrate your humanity. Glorify and enjoy God. Watch for touches of grace in your lives and....keep a sense of humor! Oh, and remember that if you give a man a fish he will eat for a day. If you teach him how to fish, he will sit in a boat drinking beer forever."

The minister winked at us, bowed his head and returned to his chair.

We opened the outside door and watched as the teenagers headed for the large purple TAG bus. They were laughing. They were dancing. They had, indeed, become talented and gifted.

Meatloaf

RUTH MANNING STOOD AT her kitchen counter chopping onions and crying. She was not crying because of the onion essence permeating the air around her, but because no matter what she cooked for dinner, her husband and son complained about it.

"I am not a bad cook," she said aloud through her tears to no one outside the window above where she was working. They are just so darned mean. Even when they eat every bite I put on their plates, they grumble and gripe.

She scraped the tiny bits of onion into a blue fiesta bowl with the edge of her knife, then began hacking at a green pepper. She threw it into the bowl along with the torn bread, ketchup, salt and pepper she had already set out.

She walked over to her avocado green refrigerator and opened the door. The light fell across her face, still wet from crying. She pushed aside some old cauliflower in a stained Tupperware container, grabbed an egg, and pulled out the hamburger. She returned to the counter, broke the egg into the blue bowl, and began stirring vigorously.

Just as she was about to tear the cellophane from the meat, she heard a car in the driveway and looked out. Her husband, Dwayne, was struggling to slide his fat belly under the steering wheel and out of the open car door.

At that moment her son, Ronald, wheeled up behind the car, his purple and orange skateboard a small propelling missile under his bent knees and protruding bottom. He slammed into the open door. His skateboard flew out from under him and landed on the hood of the car upside down, its wheels still spinning.

"A moving hood ornament," Ruth commented. "Looks kinda cute. Hmmm…that might sell real well." She chewed on her lip.

Dwayne had emerged from the car and was pulling Ronald up by both arms. They were gesturing wildly, and Ruth could hear them yelling but could not make out the words. She walked to the pantry, took out a can of Ken-L-Ration, and pulled a can opener from the drawer. By the time her husband and son had slammed the kitchen door, still screaming at one another, she had the meatloaf in the oven.

Intervention

L<small>ISA AWOKE SUDDENLY AND</small> rolled over, marks from the vinyl lounge chair lining her cheek, then wiped the saliva pooled at the corner of her mouth.

"Geez, I must have been drooling in my sleep," she said aloud.

Dizzily she pulled herself up and stared out at the empty pool, shady and clear in the late sunlight. A small, brick, two-story apartment building stared back at her beyond the pool. As she dropped her head into her hands, she noticed the empty thermos beside her chair. Oh yes, that was it, those damned screwdrivers.

It was coming back to her now. She had made the bed, straightened the apartment, started a load of laundry, showered and headed for the small tidy kitchen where she opened the refrigerator and removed a carton of orange juice. After filling her stainless steel thermos half full, she reached under the sink and pushed around the detergents and cleaners until she located the vodka. She added some to the orange juice and carefully replaced the bottle.

"Aha," she said to no one, shaking the thermos. "The other wives will enjoy these at the pool. We can have a little fun in the sun."

None of the other women had taken her up on her offer.

Lisa looked at her watch. God, it was almost five. John would be coming home soon. She gathered the empty thermos and her towel and slowly made her way to 3-B. "I'd better get dinner made so he can eat before he has a chance to bitch at me about finding another job."

Her job at Tiny Tots Daycare had been more than enjoyable. Having a degree in early education, she was comfortable playing with the children, hoisting them into swings, reading stories to them, and cuddling them when they cried for their mommies. However, the director, Mrs. Knowles, did not like her. A personality conflict was what she told John. He called Mrs. Knowles then, after Lisa was fired.

"Lisa," he looked at her sadly, "it was not a personality conflict. It was nothing personal at all. Mrs. Knowles told me she smelled liquor on your breath at work."

"See, I told you! She doesn't like me. Why else would she make up something like that?" Lisa walked away.

Many fights and arguments had erupted between them since that conversation. John remained calm when he pleaded with Lisa to get help.

"Even Laurie told me you smelled of alcohol when you met her for lunch last week. She said you acted muddled," John said to her. She just looked past him and shook her head. Laurie was her best friend. Whose side was she on, anyway?

Cool air rushed against her when she opened her apartment door. She shivered, hurried into the kitchen, and pulled out her favorite cookbook. Several scraps of paper fluttered to the floor—her recipe markers for dishes requiring wine.

"Okay, here we go…lemons, capers, butter, white wine! I'd better chill a bottle. John will enjoy it with this chicken piccata." She hummed while she put together the ingredients.

A short while and long hot shower later, Lisa pulled on her comfortable faded jeans and blue spandex halter top that John said made her look sexy.

Returning to the kitchen, she pulled out the wine, carefully opened and poured it to the rim of one of their best crystal goblets— her favorite wedding present. "I'll just sip one glass while I cook," she said to herself.

Salad vegetables were chopped, water was boiling for the rice and butter was sizzling for the chicken when she realized her goblet was empty.

Pouring another full glass, she lifted the lid of the pan and added a splash to the chicken. Napkins, plates and silver had been put out when she looked over at the counter and saw the empty bottle.

"Oh well," she said aloud, "I'll just tell John I used most of it to cook." She took out another bottle, hastily turned it through the ice bin and opened it.

Just then Lisa heard John coming in the front door.

"Hi!" she yelled merrily. "How was your day?"

But it wasn't just John who walked into the kitchen. Her parents, her older sister, Anne, and brother-in-law, James, all followed. And behind them, a man she had never seen before. Her eyes widened. "Oh, Lordy, what's wrong? Has someone died? What are you all doing here?"

It was her mother who answered, "No one has died, Lisa. Let's sit down in the living room."

"Whew, thank God," Lisa said. "You scared me half to death." They left the kitchen. Lisa turned off the burners under their dinner and shouted after them, "I'm on my way. Anyone want a drink? I have just opened a lovely bottle of chilled sauvignon blanc." She refilled her goblet, grabbed the bottle and followed them into the living room.

Prey

A BEIGE VAN, PROCLAIMING ITSELF "Kent's Kenyan Tours," careened wildly before slamming to a stop behind our army green Land Rover. When the dust settled itself back onto the dirt road, five wiggling tourists clad in safari suits and broad-brimmed Indiana Jones hats disembarked in a noisy cluster. They scurried around, not unlike the flies that were circling in droning mobs around the fresh kill we had all stopped to behold. The flies, however, had no cameras flapping around their necks.

We sat atop our open sunroof, my three friends and I, along with Pocket, our Samburu scout, whose long tight braids and entire face were painted with bright orange powdered clay. He looked resplendent in his legion of beaded bracelets and necklaces. Under the scarlet cloth tucked at his waist he wore nothing, a fact I discovered when I turned to look up at him from the back seat our first day out on safari. His ears were stretched low by the weight of large round corks inserted into his lobes, and his bountiful white teeth gleamed when he smiled.

He was not smiling now. In fact, his frown was menacing, and the muscles in his arms flexed as he held tightly to his long feathered spear. He was watching the Kent Kenyan Tour folks creep deliberately and silently toward the bloody mass that had, only a few moments before, been a large, clumsy, shy water buffalo. Our group had observed three female lions mount him and bring him down slowly as he tried to stumble on. They noisily began ripping flesh. The water buffalo succumbed silently.

Pocket said something to David, our British guide, who was sitting in the driver's seat smoking a Marlboro. He spoke in Swahili, and David turned away from the kill to see where he was pointing. "Bloody, goddamned fools."

The tourists crept on. One of them inched ahead of the others right beside our jeep, his camera whirring and clicking. The rest of the group followed behind him, keeping their distance. Their guide stood in the road, leaning against the hood of the van, his arms crossed in front of his chest. His mirrored sunglasses flashed in the sunlight.

The pride had grown to five long supple females, who stared silently and backed away from the kill as a huge stately male lion trotted toward them. He appeared from nowhere, regal and dignified. When he had settled himself on his haunches and torn out the tenderest piece of the buffalo's thigh, the females joined him.

Two cubs sat outside the eating frenzy, awaiting the scraps that would cover the ground once the adults had filled their bellies. The adults looked directly up at us between bites, their whiskers and claws dripping blood and torn flesh, their yellow eyes piercing us to the center of our souls, or so the Kenyans told us. I doubted it not.

Their gazes shifted. The tourist who was creeping ahead of his own pack caught their attention. Suddenly, Pocket jumped straight up into the air. His rubber tire sandals splatted as he landed gracefully on the hood of our jeep. He drew back his arm and released his spear deftly and quickly. The lioness was faster.

She was standing over the screaming man, holding him to the ground with her large front paws. She ripped out his throat. He emitted a tortuous, gurgling howl, writhed spasmodically, and grew still. Pocket's spear was lodged firmly in her side, its bright feathers the only part that had not penetrated her body. Just as she stumbled and fell over, one of her pride took the man's foot firmly in her mouth and dragged it over to the sitting cubs. They began to eat greedily, batting at one another, and she returned to the water buffalo, burying her head deep into its side.

The man's hat lay on the ground and beside it, his camera, its lens shattered—a lonely, wounded eye beseeching the vast African sky. It was a Nikon.

No one spoke of the kill that night as we sat

around the candle-lit dinner table in the dining tent. The only sounds echoing through the immense, merciless dark were the screeching of frightened monkeys as they warned their families of approaching predators, and pop after pop of corks being pried out of many bottles of South African red wine.

Pocket squatted beside the fire outside the tent, carving and fashioning a new spear.

Rescue

I REJOICE IN THE NAKED flesh of the living. As I
climb up my ladder chair, I look closely at my own
body, uncovered except for the bright orange, polyester bathing trunks that girdle my manhood. I am
the color of Colombian coffee with a healthy splash
of rich cream. The fine hairs on my arms and legs
have turned blonde and seem to reflect the bright
sunlight in each tiny shaft.

This is the third of three months I spend each
summer immersing myself in sunshine, light, sand,
never-ending waves, and breathing bodies. The aqua
sea bestows upon me the pulse of life—waves that
roll, crash, or tumble onto the beach in constant
rhythm, making me believe the earth itself breathes
here.

Manipulating lifeless bodies, contemplating their

existence below in a place deep, silent and far less forgiving than the sea when it rages savagely, consumes me during the remaining nine months of the year.

Even the rebirth of spring offers no solace for me. It is here on the beach that I reclaim my link to everything vital. I celebrate all of it.

The old folks arrive first, early in the mornings. Old men, their knobby, white, hairless knees and sunken chests excite me, as do the old women, who are well-oiled under big straw hats. Glittering rhinestones twinkle on their red and blue sunglasses with each turn of their smiling, wrinkled faces. They will all leave around noon, pushing themselves off their chairs carefully and slowly, to seek refuge from the sun's high rays and claim both sandwiches without sand and a long afternoon snooze.

Joining the old people a little later in the mornings are the matrons, those delectable females carrying brightly colored towels and fold-up aluminum chairs, with toddlers swinging plastic buckets and shovels. Many of them are pregnant again, overgrown with ripening life. They display infinite patience with the rowdy young ones who run ahead of them, kicking sand and squealing, their sturdy, sun-screened legs pumping wildly. I, by the grace of God, have had only a few of these small bodies to prepare. I cannot reconcile any ending to such a vigorous beginning.

These young mothers lounge in their chairs, intersperse their chatting with watching the sand sift between their painted toenails and crossing their legs in an effort to remain seductive.

Arriving next are the taut, hard, smooth forms of young men and women, their eyelids heavy with the long, untroubled, weekend sleep of youth. They display their bodies immodestly, confidently, and plunge into both the water and their red and white Playmate coolers with rippling muscles and graceful recklessness. I glorify each and every one of them, while offering a prayer that they will be spared an early end to such beautiful innocence. Was it only a few short years ago that I, too, was so unaware of my mortality?

A slight, golden-haired girl looks up at me. She waves and smiles. Her teeth are straight and white. She bends over to push a volleyball pole deep into the sand, allowing me to enjoy the full tops of her magnificent young breasts as they spill out of her tiny yellow bikini top.

I wave back, and then continue my inventory of the souls on my watch, none of whom have yet made me fight for their lives in the tides and treacherous undercurrents that could easily pull them into the sea.

I never for one minute underestimate this huge expanse of throbbing water and what lies beneath it. I am determined only to preserve these dear people in their precarious clutch of life and keep their bodies stretching, laughing, eating, loving, breathing, working, playing, and being.

No, I am not your regular bronzed, hard-bodied, streaked pony-tailed or crew-cut all American lifeguard, lounging high above the beach in my own vanity. I am Howie Bailey, only heir to Bailey's Funeral Home, right here in this small seaside town of Beaufort, South Carolina, a business started of necessity when Southern Infantry sought refuge, unsuccessfully, around here during the Civil War. My great great grandfather was forced into caring for the dead, lest currents and winds handed them to the elements, denying loved ones a chance for closure.

"Someone has to do this job," my own father's southern drawl rang in my ears many times when I was deciding what to do with my life. "The fine people in this town depend on us to carry out the task of death with grace and dignity. We are counting on *you*, son, to uphold our tradition."

So now I spend most of the year locked in the small, white, sterile room behind the kitchen of the home in which I grew up. I fill bodies with fluids that plump and unline their faces, so their loved ones are tricked into believing they are restive and peaceful in their satin-lined eternity beds.

I am the creator of illusions that block minds from a reality that would fill them with torment. I am caretaker for the defunct—keeper of lifelessness.

I answer this somber call with grace and mercy, and wait patiently for the summer so I can answer another call—one that immerses me in the joyous, dynamic celebration of life.

By the way, now that I am in charge of Howard S. Bailey's Funeral Home, I have changed the ad in the yellow pages. It used to say, "Tender Care for your Departed Loved Ones." It now reads, "Glorify Life. We Will Take Care of Death. Closed June, July, and August."

The Fall

ADAM REALIZED QUITE SOON after taking a bite of the apple Eve offered him that he really could not fly. He had been peering intently over the edge of a steep cliff, arms outstretched, when he heard God shout, "Adam, what do you think you are doing?"

Terror and alarm filled his newly formed body. He lost his balance and plunged headfirst over the side of the mountain. He thrashed about wildly, flailing and flapping his arms, just as he had seen the birds do. His efforts failed. He was, however, fortunate enough to land atop a lovely flowering fruit tree in the garden, where he frowned and looked skyward.

"You scared me. Why did you yell at me? I was only trying to fly like the birds. Eve has learned to swim like the fishes in the sea, so why can't I learn to soar in the sky?" He sounded like a petulant child.

Now God had parted the fluffy clouds when one of His staff informed Him something was amiss below. He watched Adam clamor to hang on to the treetop. Its lovely foliage quivered and shook as he struggled.

"Adam, you are not a bird. Who in the garden gave you the idea you could fly?"

"That snake down there," Adam answered, pointing at the lush garden.

"Snake?" God shook His head in amazement. The heavens rumbled.

"Well, what do you know? A serpent! I thought perhaps Satan would appear in the form of a crow or a vulture, but certainly not a snake."

The firmament became silent for a moment. Then God spoke again. "Oh well. Maybe it is better this way. At least he cannot fly."

"You mean that snake down there who told Eve to eat the apple is Satan?" Adam asked, his voice cracking. He was clutching the high branches tightly.

"He told her the apple would make us understand everything, so she took the apple and went down to the sea. She came back and told me she had been swimming with the fishes. Then I took a bite. We had no idea it was Satan! No wonder he laughed when I climbed up the mountain to fly."

"Yes, indeed, Satan has slithered into my garden," God said to Adam. "I did not expect him so soon. Now I will really be busy. Why did you let him and Eve talk you into taking a bite of the apple?"

"Well, I thought if we could understand everything, I could at least learn to fly. Eve learned how to swim, didn't she? After she took a bite," Adam reasoned.

"You had all that you needed, Adam," God told him gently. "If I had intended you to fly, I would have made you a bird. Then you would have only the qualities a bird has. You are so much more than that."

"Yeah, you sure are more than just a bird. You are a birdbrain," came a hissing, laughing voice from below. Satan was coiled up at the bottom of the tree. Eve stood close by, holding a glass of wine and listening closely to the conversation.

"You tricked me!" Adam looked down and shouted at the serpent. "You said we would have power over everything when you gave Eve that apple! Now, look at me. I am stuck up in this tree, and I still can't fly. And I can't swim, either. At least Eve can swim. Or is that one of your tricks, too, you ol' slimy snake?"

Satan cackled and wound his scaly body around and around the tree trunk. He looked up at Adam with his slanty eyes. "Nope, not a trick. She taught herself to swim, you foolish mortal. She knew right away how the water would feel against her skin. She had sense enough not to jump off a cliff, but she sure did get huffy. Just look what she did to God's lovely plump grapes after she threw the apple core at me! She trompled them into pulp!"

"And look, Adam," Eve chimed in. "Smashed grapes make wine! It is really tasty!" She laughed.

"Maybe you can make something good out of our mistake, too. Climb down and share it with me!"

"I can't climb down. That no good, no shouldered creature is curled around the bottom of this tree, just waiting to trick me again," Adam whined.

Then God blew a huge, swirling wind toward the garden, and Adam twirled right out of the tree. He landed at Eve's feet, scooted quickly away from the coiling snake, then stood up and rubbed his bare bottom. "Ouch."

Eve handed him the wine, then turned to Satan. "We'd ask you to join us, but you have no hands. Besides, you have disrupted our existence enough, and you know what can happen when I am angry."

The snake looked at her warily and hissed, "I am leaving, but I will be back, you can be sure." He slithered sulkily away.

Adam took a sip of the wine and looked up at God. "I feel certain we haven't seen the last of You either. Maybe I will be able to fly when I become an angel. Until then, we can drink wine. And play in the sea, if Eve will teach me to swim. Cheers." He lifted his glass. God laughed. The clouds closed up, leaving only a cottony bit of fluff in a sparkling blue sky to oversee His magnificent creation.

Specs

OUR ONLY SON CAME over for dinner one night last month. He said he had something to tell us, and since we don't see him too often now that he is out of college and on his own, I cooked his favorite dinner. He lives over in Bennetsville, only about fifteen miles from us out here on the farm, but we don't get over there like we used to, now that they built that new Piggly Wiggly and movie rental place out here on the by-pass.

I am a woman with a more liberated way of thinking than Harold, who is my husband, so when our son told us he was gay, just blurted it right out between bites of his chicken and dumplings, I didn't get angry. Harold sure did, as you can imagine. He yelled and cursed and asked our son who in the world had molested him and made him that way, along with about a hundred other questions. He said that no boy of his was light on his feet and that we should have known that someone would lead him astray when we let him go on over to USC instead of taking over our farm.

Anyway, our boy stayed calm, he always does, and said that nothing had happened to him; that it was just decided for him by Mother Nature and he had known it for a long time before college. Now like I said, I didn't get mad. I may not understand it too well, but I knew right then and there I would choose to keep him in my life. I didn't care who or how he loved. Harold still won't go to visit him.

I think about his childhood a lot nowadays. In fact, just yesterday I pulled open the top drawer of the antique pine bureau in his bedroom, which is now my sewing room, and right there under the purple and white checked scraps of my kitchen curtain material, I found his very first pair of glasses. You know those black rimmed plastic ones kids used to wear when they first got glasses? I always thought they made him look like a miniature Roy Orbison.

Anyway, the first thing I did was hold those spectacles up to my eyes, though they didn't fit my face, and look around at everything. I think I was hoping to see my son's vision of the world when he was growing up. So I sat right down there on the old, worn out, braided oval rug and peered around. And wouldn't you know it, I did begin to see.

My memories came tumbling out. I recalled that when his father forced him to play Little League, he ducked each and every time a ball was hit to him in center field. It never bothered him; he just let the ball scoot on past him. That's when we got him these little glasses, but by then the season was over.

When I looked at his books all lined up straight and still as little soldiers right there on his corner bookcase, my mind went back to the times he'd sit for hours and hours during the summer on the upstairs landing window seat with a pile of those books beside him.

I used to marvel at his concentration, especially when the boys from up the road, Ted and Larry Atkins, came over to run through the sprinklers in our front yard. Their parents never dug a well, so there was always a water shortage up there if the summer was dry. Now I can't help but wonder if he was admiring those young male bodies even then.

I used to thank my lucky stars that he wasn't aggressive or rowdy. Those rough and tumble boyhoods that included lots of trips to the emergency room were unknown to us. Harold always complained that he was the one who had to bait the hooks when he took our son fishing, but he forgot about it when those fish were fried up and waiting on a platter for his dinner.

I took a long look at his stuffed animals sitting on the old green beanbag chair in the corner. They're mostly bears, but there's a black flop-eared dog he named Scooter, after our real dog, a black lab that died of old age when our son was just about to graduate from high school. I never knew a person's eyes could hold so many tears. He gave the sweetest eulogy when we buried old Scooter out behind the barn. He had us all sobbing, even Harold.

I stood up then and looked at myself in the small pine mirror over his bureau and tried to see the mother that I was. The week after we brought him home from the hospital, I thought I would never sleep again. Really, I don't think mothers ever sleep soundly once those small people are part of their lives. I mopped his face over and over with a cold washcloth, sometimes all night long, when he had a fever. I could tell when his breathing changed, even a room away. I was the one he clung to when he was scared, the one who walked him to the school bus every morning, the one who reminded him to put on these glasses so he could read the board, and the one who openly admired his gentle ways with each and every stray cat or dog that wandered into the yard.

I felt silly, looking at myself through those small specs. But I did see something, sure enough. I saw a woman who wouldn't do one thing differently than I did it. And I'm going to insist that Harold look through these glasses himself. I think he will do it, too. Just last night he asked me when I plan to go over to Bennetsville again and have dinner with our boy. He said he'd seen an ad for a used tractor over there that sounded pretty good. I have a feeling he's about to be blessed with insight.

Trenches

Mama quit singing in the choir that year. Oh, she still went with us to church on Sundays, but her voice in the Mt. Calvary Baptist Church Choir never rang out in praise again.

She told folks that with my brother, Davy, gone, Daddy needed her help with the milking every evening, which was a lie. I took over his job in the barn. Daddy and I didn't argue though. We knew she just couldn't do the milking or attend choir practice since that was the time of day when those Vietnam War pictures came on the evening news. She even moved our small Zenith TV to the kitchen and put it right on the counter. She didn't miss one broadcast the whole year Davy was over there.

Most nights the TV news would be over by the time Daddy and I came in to dinner.

"I didn't see my boy tonight," she'd say, passing the blue and white chipped platter stacked with fried chicken.

"Of course, you didn't!" Daddy spoke harshly, his rough calloused hand trembling as he speared his dinner. "He's out there on the front lines, not hiding in the trenches waiting for the news folks to come and take his picture! He's a man!"

"How can the army make him a man?" Mama asked then, looking out at the pasture. "Seems to me that's a job for his family, his church, and his papa, teaching him about the land and how to work it."

"Putting country first, learning how to fight and defend our freedom sure as hell made me a man!"

"Well, that war was different," Mama's voice cracked. "How can he come home a man when young folks around here are going barefoot and wearing flowers? Why, just yesterday I saw a young girl standing on the train platform waving a pathetic toy flag and chanting about peace—right smack in front of two boys in uniform with duffel bags waiting to leave. I was coming out of the A&P and what a sight it was. Our war made soldiers heroes."

&

A letter arrived telling us Davy was headed back to Ft. Bragg for debriefing and would be home in about four weeks. Mama smiled a little more often then. She'd tell us about her dreams and visions, which seemed to anger Daddy as much as her ramblings about peace and manhood.

"I see him, my own little Davy, over a vast ocean in a plane, smiling and eager to get home to us. He is wearing overalls, not a uniform, because he wants to be a farmer again. I just don't understand why he needs 'debriefing.' All he needs is us, his family. I think the army should just send him straight home."

Mama's dream was wrong. Davy returned to the farm, sure enough, but he never took on any more farming. Almost every morning Mama woke up and found him, clinging fetal-like to the old oak tree in the backyard. I would hear her screaming and run to the window. There she'd be, trying to pull him to his feet, tears streaming down both their faces. Seems Davy would sleepwalk right out there, fighting off Mama and Daddy if they tried to wake him out of it. Daddy would sometimes drag him out to the barn, but he'd just run away, throw himself down on the ground and cover his head with his arms.

One night their voices drifted up the stairs. "Where do I put it, Daddy?" I thought Davy was talking about his cigarette at first, since Mama didn't let him smoke in the house and I could smell his Lucky Strike. "I saw young men, like myself, with their very own legs beside them, cuddling them like they were stuffed animals or something. We always put their limbs on the stretcher with them, telling them they'd get them back on, but we knew they wouldn't. Then we'd come into a village and realize that the trees were full of body parts—women's and children's, too. Help me, Daddy."

I knew that if Davy were asking Mama for her

help, she'd take him in her arms and try to comfort him. Daddy didn't do that though.

"Put it where all men do, son! Right in the front of your mind so you never forget what it is like to be a soldier!! Now stop this sissy talk and get on up to bed. We got to start early tomorrow."

Davy didn't start early the next day. I was in the middle of a dream about bloody children when I heard Daddy wail. Davy had made his way out to the old oak tree again. He wasn't curled up under it this time. He was swinging from it, his very own bed sheets holding him up.

The Mr. Calvary Baptist Church Choir sang a splendid assortment of Mama's favorite hymns at Davy's funeral, including "Amazing Grace." Too bad she wasn't there to hear them.

The Stripper

Jamie dossman stands at the gray granite-topped center island in an immaculate black-and-white tiled kitchen gently spooning tiny dabs of white goat cheese on the tips of endive lettuce leaves. His professional and personal partner, Tom, a young thin man in his early twenties, stands next to him, topping each white dab with a whole black walnut.

They are smiling, conversing softly with one another, appearing unflappable despite the line of jiggling, singing, middle-aged women winding its way through the kitchen in the bunny hop style that was fashionable in the sixties. Instead of raising each of their right legs, then left legs in unison, they are each wiggling their brightly-clad hips in Capri pants, one directly in front of the other, and doing a sort of short-stepped bump and grind.

Boney M's steel drum Caribbean band is blaring
from the CD player in the next room, its rendition of
Yellow Bird enhanced happily and loudly from this
wiggling, dancing, joyful and very drunk worm of
women who are now heading into the dining room.
Botanical prints bounce jauntily on the linen-tex-
tured walls as they turn the corner.

A rich brown smell of roasting meat, an expensive
cut, unfurls around them. On they go, collapsing into
a heap of laughter and chubby bottoms right there on
the Oriental carpet. Mrs. Todd, leader of the line, has
managed to hold aloft her frosty goblet of Jamaican
rum punch and takes a long swig just as her ample
body spills out around her.

"Well, that's it," Jamie says to Tom in the kitchen.
He is full figured himself, older than Tom and heftier,
looking like an island cook tonight in his baggy turquoise and lime green tropical fish print chef pants.
"Time to carve the tenderloin. This group is in need
of protein."

He grabs a huge black oven glove, removes the
sizzling meat, its life juices pink and leaking out into
the French copper roasting pan. He places it gently
on the counter, and Tom begins to carve, arrang-
ing each slice artfully and slightly overlapping on a
bright pottery platter.

"Yeah, and the stripper will be here soon," Tom
answers, still creating. "That'll be a hoot again, I'm
sure. What kind of costume did our lovely hostess
choose tonight? Something Caribbean, I'm sure."

"No, believe it or not, there was only one kind

available. Must be a lot of bachelorette parties out there tonight. It's a cop," Jamie tells him. They giggle. The male strippers are their favorite part of each catering job here at Mrs. Todd's.

The doorbell rings. There is much huffing and puffing and hysterical laughter as the ladies struggle to their feet in the dining room. Mrs. Todd's voice is the next thing they hear.

"She sounds just like Blanche Devereaux on *The Golden Girls* and damn, he's early. I was hoping to get some solid food in them before he started." Jamie tells Tom.

"Oh my, Occifer, don't you look cute tonight!" Mrs. Todd exclaims slurringly, as a police officer in uniform steps through the doorway, removing his hat and looking sternly at the group of twittering women.

"Why, your badge evens looks real this time!" she goes on. She fingers it, and reaches around behind him to rub his butt. "And...as usual, your tush is nice and tight. Gladys, change the CD! Put on 'The Stripper,' and let's get on with it!" Gladys makes a beeline for the den, and Mrs. Todd takes the officer by the hand.

They follow. So does the rest of the group. The officer's eyes have become large, and he is sputtering, but makes no effort to resist her. Sexy jazz trumpets fill the air, and the women begin to clap in time to them. "Take it off! Real slowly!" they hoot and holler, punching each other and forming a ring around him.

Jamie and Tom have come in to watch and are standing in the doorway grinning foolishly. Tom is holding a platter of red tuna squares topped with swirls of green wasabi. Jamie has filled a silver tray with fresh refills of rum punch, each glass glistening with moisture and sprouting a paper umbrella.

The policeman is standing perfectly still, his mouth hanging open. He is covering his crotch with both hands as the women reach into their pockets and pull out bills in varying denominations, waving them under his nose, their fingers tickling his chest and pulling at his belt loops. One is fingering his holster.

How Jamie hears the doorbell amidst the uproarious laughter and deafening sensuous music is unclear, but hear it he does. He heads down the front hall, still clutching the silver tray. A police officer is standing on the threshold as Jamie opens the door.

He swaggers in, swinging his hips seductively, winks at Jamie and takes a glass of rum punch. A dark brown pony tail peeks out from under the back of his cap. He is young, tanned, well-muscled and tall. Polka dot bikini briefs show through his polyester uniform pants as he begins to undulate. His badge reads "Party Favors, Inc.," and his gun is silver plastic.

"Oh, my God," Jamie gasps. "Mrs. Todd, you better get in here!" he yells down the hall. The phone rings. Not waiting to see if she heard him, he runs in the kitchen, grabs it out of its cradle. His rum punches topple and tip.

"I told you the last time that if you ever had another loud party, I would call the police." It's Mr. Graves from downstairs. Jamie turns toward the den just in time to see Mrs. Todd twirling a uniform above her head. The first cop is standing in his issue-gray underwear, hands still covering his privates.

The Purchase

AN OLD MEXICAN MAN shuffled down the dirt road. A fat brown dog followed him. Both were wearing straw hats, the dog's tied loosely at his neck. They turned into an art gallery. The old man took off his hat. The dog did not.

"Hola, old man!" the gringo sitting behind the desk at the back of the store said and stood up. "You have come for your painting? You have made up your mind?"

"Sí, we think today is the day. Could you please put them side by side once again on your big stand?"

The gringo disappeared behind an arched doorway. He returned quickly with two notebook-sized pieces and displayed them together on a tall wooden easel. The subjects were the same—watercolor renderings of a ferocious wave crashing upon the sand. A setting sun behind the Pacific lent hues of mauve and orange to one. A blazing sun sent sparkles through the breaking foam in the deep blue of the other.

The old man pulled a pair of glasses from the front pocket of his short-sleeved cotton shirt. Stuffing his hat under one arm, he leaned over and put them on the dog. Both the old man and the dog looked from one painting to the other. Their heads turned in unison, back and forth, back and forth. Then they looked at one another, and the old man nodded at the shimmering dark blue wave. He took off the dog's glasses and put them back in his pocket.

"We'll take the dark blue," he said. "We like the diamonds in the waves."

"Good choice," said the proprietor. "A violent wave should be deeply hued. It enhances the water's ruthlessness and mystery. The softer one implies innocence."

The old man shrugged. He pulled many pesos from his pants and counted them out slowly as he placed them upon the gringo's outstretched palm.

"Thank you, señor." He folded the money and placed it in his desk drawer.

"I will wrap it for you." The gallery owner pulled a large piece of brown paper off a roll on the wall and gently wrapped the painting. He handed it to the old man who bowed from the waist and headed out the door. The dog followed.

The old man and the dog turned down the dirt road that would take them home. The sun was high. The dust swirled around them. The dog stayed close, his hat brim bumping the old man's calf. A dirty white Brahma bull gnawing on brown vegetation ignored them as they walked along. Car skeletons rusting beside the road stared at them with empty windshield eyes. Scrawny Mexican dogs littered the sandy landscape with great sadness.

When the sea could be heard thrashing between the mountains, the old man and his dog turned toward the sound and came upon their own little adobe hut. They entered through the heavy wooden arched door. The old man hung both their hats on the rusty nails beside it.

He carefully unwrapped his artwork and held it aloft beside the glassless window facing the ocean. He looked from the window to the painting and back again several times. He laughed joyfully, then turned around to see if the dog agreed, but the dog was already curled up, deep in his siesta.

The Skillet

Edna looked through her kitchen window. It wasn't quite light outside yet so her image was pure, softer than the wrinkled, haggard and sagging face the mirror showed her when she looked at herself. Which certainly wasn't often these days, not with Don as sick as he was.

His illness consumed her, just like the growth eating up his insides. At least that's how Edna pictured the cancer, a huge smiling head, its long sharp teeth sinking into healthy tissue (whatever that looked like), and then spitting it out in little pieces to run away and furrow somewhere else, build a new colony.

Don's reflection, as he sat hunched over the red Formica kitchen table behind her, was blurry. The back of his bald head sitting atop his bony shoulders in his old green bathrobe reminded her of a bulb on a slender stem, tenuous and fragile, wobbly and ready to burst into bloom. She lifted the last piece of bacon from the sizzling grease and turned around.

"How many eggs do you want this morning, old man?" Old man was her pet name for Don, bestowed upon him when they were first married over thirty years ago. A new outbreak of polio spread through their small Kansas town shortly before the vaccine reached them. She remembered clearly standing in line as a young girl in the school cafeteria and being handed a small paper cup of blue liquid to drink. Her mother whispered behind her, "Drink it down, Edna. It'll keep you from being crippled like your friend, Don."

She had seen pictures of children imbedded forever in large silver tunnels on wheeled tables with only their heads visible, and squeezed her eyes shut, right then and there. "Make him just be crippled, Lord," she prayed silently. "Not in one of those awful tubes, please."

Her prayer had been answered. Don was left with only a slight limp.

"Life will be hard," he told her. "A farmer's work is never done." His father had given them ten acres adjoining their own hundred-acre farm, a wedding present to get them started. He had even built them a small, white wooden house with a wrap-around green porch that matched the shutters. There, they raised their children.

"I am very aware of how hard it is to work the land.

Just because my daddy runs a variety store doesn't mean I don't know about farming. I spent plenty of summers with Uncle Ben and Aunt Louise, don't forget. Besides, when you come in for noon dinner, we just might eat it in our bed!" She shocked herself and blushed. He laughed and hugged her tightly. "I reckon then we'd never get our chores done!"

"I'll just have one this morning," his weak voice broke her reverie. She hefted the large black iron frying pan, holding its handle with two protective oven gloves and poured the grease into a rusty Maxwell House can sitting beside the stovetop. It hissed its way down. She pushed the can back on the counter to cool and broke one egg into the pan, then turned around. He was hunched over, his head on his folded arms.

"You okay, old man?" She walked to the table and pulled out a chair, its aluminum legs scraping loudly as she slid it over next to him. He looked up, turning his head to look up at her, arms still folded on the table.

"We need new chairs," was all he said. She looked at the back of the chair she was holding and sure enough, white stuffing was poking out of a gouge in its red and white checked vinyl back. She sat down.

"Yep, we surely do. This is the last one to rip." The other three chair backs were already decorated with silver electrician tape. For some reason, it now seemed silly to her that they had tried to stuff the white cotton back into each chair. Like trying to keep life force in when, in fact, it was ready to work its way out. The kitchen table set was their first purchase. No, second. They bought a double mattress and box springs first.

Don coughed then and yellow fluid trickled out of the corner of his mouth. "I changed my mind. No eggs."

Edna grabbed a napkin from the chipped plastic rooster in front of her. She stifled a gag while she wiped his face. It smelled awful, and his skinny shoulders shook and trembled with each rattling hack. She stuffed another napkin at his chin, slid her chair back, and got up.

"No eggs. Okay, old man, I'll just turn down the fire under the skillet and then I'll help you to the sofa. News ought to be on by now. Maybe you'll feel up to eating after it's over."

She walked over to the stove, turned out the flame, pulled on her old flowered stove mitts again, and tipped the egg into the can of grease. Her reflection was gone now, the sun had come up. She looked out across their land, all one hundred and ten acres of it, now that Don's parents had passed on. Too bad their children chose city life. Still holding the skillet, she turned around and looked at her husband. His retching continued, and the spittle had puddled on his folded arms.

Edna had played softball in her youth. Her swing was accurate. And years of hard work had put muscle under all that jiggle in her upper arms. She'd put him back up in his chair. No autopsy, she was sure of that. Lloyd was their friend, as well as the local medical examiner. He would take care of Don quickly, if she asked him to. And she would. Then she'd ask him to stop by the hardware store on his way over and bring her a "For Sale" sign.

Pyramid Chest

THE CHEST OVER WHICH they bickered was, as Russ, the gallery owner and its creator described it, a work of art. Constructed of mahogany and corrugated tin, it stood about six feet tall, the drawers diminished in size going up, the largest one on the bottom. It was actually an old stepladder creatively fashioned and framed into a pyramid chest of drawers. "In New York this piece would sell immediately, and I would be building ten more," Russ told us, pulling at his gray ponytail and plopping down on a chair, long tan legs splaying out of his short shorts.

I nodded in agreement, looked around at the odd assortment of sculptures and browsers in this café style Key West art shop. A "stick your finger in a socket" spiked-haired youth wandering around on ten grubby toes of assorted nail colors with several tarnished nose rings was no more surprising than the sculpture of a man with his head up a woman's skirt. A couple, both blonde males, stood together, their arms entwined around each other's slender tight-jeaned hips. They looked adoringly at each painting, nodded, and moved on to the next. They lingered in front of the chest, both of them stroking it tenderly with their free hands. I heard the words "clever, eclectic, functional."

Anyway, I couldn't have said "no" to Harriet when she called and invited herself and Wayne, her third husband, here to Key West, where homeowners contend that houseguests and tides are one in the same – they roll in, they roll out, the full moon brings the noisiest ones, and all of them erode our sanity. She was my college roommate and, although we hadn't seen each other in twenty years, our communal living and four years of hard work, partying, and growing had secured a connection.

The older version of Harriet was only mildly changed. She was still a tall, gangly, frizzy-haired brunette. We had enjoyed a perfunctory two Bloody Mary, Key West lunch with Wayne, her little, round, balding husband, whose knobby knees and bony ankles struggled to support him. His white socks and hiking boots aided in the effort. He seemed pleasant enough, despite the fact that he and Harriet had chosen matching flowered Hawaiian shirts for our excursion to Front Street. Harriet's long, green plastic earrings matched both her flip-flops and her vinyl handbag.

I glanced at Wayne, who was on his knees trying to look up the skirt of the woman in the sculpture. Harriet walked over to the chest, heaved her shiny bag from her right to left arm, and began pulling out the drawers.

"I really need this chest of drawers," she slammed a drawer shut and turned to Wayne and me.

"You don't need that thing, Harriet," he rolled his eyes, struggled to his feet, joints cracking.

"Need? You are right, Wayne. I only need air, water and food. I like this thing and I want to buy it. Come here and let me show you how deep and roomy these drawers are."

"As deep and roomy as yours?" He found himself extremely amusing and began guffawing. His silliness was contagious.

The male partners turned in unison, staring at the three of us. They giggled. So did I. Russ looked over, shrugged, and went back to playing with his hair.

"Shut up, Wayne. Come here. I want to show you this thing up close."

"And I have something to show you up close, Harriet, the bottom of the ocean." We were all on a roll, now. Even Russ let go of his hair and covered his mouth with his hand. It could not stifle his laughter.

Wayne and Harriet were hurling dangerous looks at one another. "Let's get another drink and talk this over." I offered, turning for the door. They ignored me.

Wayne's jaw began twitching. He shifted his

weight from foot to foot, doing sort of a booted, skinny leg two-step. Harriet glared at the rest of us in our hilarity, snapped open her shiny purse, produced a gold credit card, and waved it defiantly over her head. She turned to Russ, "Do you ship?"

Before he could answer her, Wayne hefted the sexy sculpture one-handed and hollered, "Sure he ships. Might as well ship this, too, while we're shipping. We can set it on top of the damned chest."

The-spike haired girl turned suddenly and started out the door. Just as she stepped outside onto the sidewalk, there came a collision of astonishing force. She smacked loudly, headlong, into a young, half-naked, dark-skinned boy.

We turned quickly enough to see them go down, a flailing tangle of suntan and colored toenails. What we did not see was his purple and orange skateboard sailing in a high curved arc right through the door of this quaint Key West art gallery, setting its course directly for the erotic statue Wayne held in the air.

Such a violent union was, in itself, a work of art. Pieces of orange and purple fiberglass, small black wheels still spinning, the tiny female head staring lifelessly at the ceiling, the man's body from shoulders down, legs still sitting in the chair, arms shattered; her skirt was, however, still intact. Wayne leaned over and picked it up gingerly, still looking under it for the man's head.

And...since Harriet had been facing the door, she had ducked, and lost her balance. There she sat, crumbled in a heap and stunned, beneath the chest, its smallest drawer perched at an angle atop her frizzy hair, the yellow vinyl strap of her shoulder bag firmly entwined in the drawer's mahogany handle.

I pulled out my checkbook.

Reverie

I THINK SHE IS ENLIGHTENED—COMICALLY engaged in the process of life while navigating her spiritual journey. This is her latest journal entry. What do you think?

—*Slept until the last possible moment. Dreams immerse us in our own reality. Mine is the best.*

—*Forgive everyone. It frees you to let God run the universe.*

—*Gulped a cup of coffee. It failed to jump start my reflexes.*

—*Sad songs do not care who they make cry.*

—*Did not quite hear what my family was saying to me. It required great effort to locate my keys and sunglasses. Which reminded me that I want to be re-incarnated as Tom Cruise's sunglasses in my next life. Would like to live close to that smile.*

—*Happy songs love it when they make folks shag.*

—*Tried not to knock off the side mirrors while backing out of the garage – a daily concern when I pull out to drive my twelve year old daughter to school.*

—*Change is the only constant in life.*

—*Endured 93.2, the rock station, until she disembarked, then switched to the news. What it was I do not recall.*

—*Label nothing. It leaves you unprepared for dealing with what you do not know.*

—*Pretended I was invisible so other parents in carpool line could not see how disheveled I looked. Middle age does nothing for the face of a woman.*

—*Manifest all that you are.*

—*Imagined I was a character in a Stephen King end of the world novel. How would I survive alone? At least there would be no traffic.*

—*God is big enough to tolerate anger and compassionate enough to understand it.*

—*Arrived home. Read the comics, Ann Landers, and the obituaries. I knew no one who had passed on yesterday.*

—*Rotate your head to get another view of the world.*

—*Went to visit my mother-in-law at the nursing home. The nurses behind the round nursing station told me she had just wheeled up in her chair and ordered a Bloody Mary. "Does it look like we're running a bar here?"*

—*Humanity may be our Creator's ongoing experiment. That's why He had to invent grace.*

—*Visited a friend whose husband just had surgery. She grabbed my arm and told me she threw wine in her brother-in-law's face at a wedding over the weekend. "Red or white?" I asked.*

—*Chase not the setting sun to prolong warmth and light. Plunge, instead, into the darkness. You will feel better about yourself when you navigate through it and find the sun just coming up on the other side.*

—*Sat down at the computer. Tried to write but kept losing the left half of my efforts.*

—*It is not what we experience in life, but how we respond to those experiences.*

—*Chartered a course through the thorns on my rosebushes. Gathered enough for a small bouquet. Put it on the kitchen table where I knew it would soon get lost in homework.*

—*Life is a turbulent sea, pounding itself against immobile rocks, then writhing and slithering down into the swirling foam, only to explode its way up again.*

—*Picked up my daughter from hockey practice. Tried to explain why the Junior League is not a beginning ballet class. Also tried to explain time management.*

—*Learn and practice detachment. It comes in handy during family chaos.*

—*Finished dinner and dishes. Fed the dog, happily escaped upstairs to read. Privacy was nonexistent. Too many voices calling, "Mom."*

—*We carry the weight of the day upon our back. That is why night time makes our burdens heavier to bear—the stars are weighing down the sky.*

—*Wearily turned out the light. As Victor Hugo (I think it was) said, "Go to sleep in peace. God is awake."*

Revival

"NEVER MARRY A MAN who gets religion late," my mama always told me. She usually said this as we were leaving the Belle Grade Baptist Church Sunday mornings, after I had spent a full hour staring at Danny Denton.

I never heard a word Reverend Jacobs said, but I sure knew how to slow down my breathing so as not to call attention to my lust for Danny. He'd swagger into the service, followed by his muscled father, Donald Denton, owner of Denton's Plumbing, who worked out of a white van with those exact words printed on it.

Mr. Denton would nudge him in the back. I could see the Lucky Strikes box outlined under the old gray blazer his father had forced him to put over his rolled up sleeved white t-shirt. I thought he looked like James Dean. Acted like him, too, all cool and confident, danger and sex oozing right out of his skin.

"Why does it matter when he gets it, as long as he gets it?" I asked her one morning. The sun was bouncing off the chrome bumpers of the parked cars and pick-up trucks lined up along the green church yard. We were squinting going down the concrete steps.

"Well, the later it hits them, the harder they get it. They get real zealous like those reformed drinkers, ranting and raving and all. I don't think you got to worry about that though, girl. The one you're a pantin' after most likely ain't gonna get it at all, early or late."

"Oh, mama, he will."

And he did—right before we got married and right after he served time for robbing Ronnie's Texaco out on Okeechobee Road. He worked alongside his daddy during the day and went to "Tent Preaching" and "Redemption of Souls" classes at the Revival Missionary Seminary over the county line in Okeechobee at night. Most "wanna be" tent preachers had to earn a living during the day, since revival preaching didn't bring in enough to live on or raise kids on, which is what we planned to do.

I went to work at the Piggly Wiggly to help out while he learned plumbing and preaching. I knew we'd have to travel when he started his revivals, so every penny helped. I put half my earnings in a canning jar on the kitchen counter right next to the mail, so when the Sears Roebuck catalogue came in, I could mark the page with the dress on it that I wanted, then look at the money I'd saved to buy it with. I'd have to look nice at the meetings, being the preacher's wife. He'd come home at night, all worn out. I'd meet him at the door.

"How's my preaching plumber?" I'd tease him, pull him close, feeling all sexy. "Let me take care of your pipes for once and you'll know you've got religion!"

He'd glare at me when I talked like that, give me a proper preacher hug and turn on the overhead light so he could hunch over his books at the kitchen table. I'd go to bed lonely and watch TV, and was usually sound asleep by the time he tiptoed in.

Anyway, we never did have those children I wanted. Danny finished his school and sure enough, he got to be a tent revival preacher. I felt right spiteful, but set up and took down those folding chairs time after time with a smile on my face. "Do the Lord's work in good cheer," he'd tell me.

Danny created himself a real following. His sermons on the sins of drinking, adultery, envy, greed, pride and every one of Satan's evils you could think of, drew big crowds. People loved hearing him. People loved him.

"Come forth, brothers and sisters!" he'd holler into the microphone. "And let the holy stain of Jesus' blood save you from the vile thoughts and deeds that Satan himself spills into your life!"

Lots of churches in those counties would send

their own choirs to sway and praise right along with him. Their brightly colored robes were a joyful sight to behold and I never got tired of all those faithful voices raised in songs, "Oh Happy Day" and "Shall We Gather At The River," just to name a few. Every single one of them touched my heart.

"I just love that tent music," I'd say to Danny. "I'll pray that you grow to love more than just the music," he'd answer me.

One night last spring I slipped silently through the flap at the very back of the tent. I walked to the hilltop behind it and looked down. The wind had billowed it up just like a big white hot air balloon, glowing in the soft moonlight, straining at the ropes and eager for take off. A balloon ride up to God, I thought. All that hot air of those bellowing, fainting, and righteous souls are sure to make it float right up to heaven.

I kept on walking, right down to the two-lane road toward the Swaying Palms Motel, where we stayed when our revival came to Polatka Springs. Danny liked to be within walking distance from the tent so he could practice his sermon out loud on the way.

I put my old army green duffel bag on the bed and folded my faded flowery dresses. "I won't leave him a note. I'll just call him when I get where I'm going," I said out loud. I turned out the lights and watched the blinking pink neon sign reflecting in the dreary window. Then I walked right down the road again, swinging my duffel, which felt much lighter than I thought it would.

A light-colored Chevrolet roared past me. Then I saw its brake lights as it stopped and pulled off to the side. I ran to catch up to it. I was out of breath when I leaned in the window the driver had lowered.

"Need a lift? Hey, I know you. You're Reverend Denton's wife!" Her smile was huge, her teeth gleamed from the lights on the dashboard. Darn if it wasn't Dorthea Lewis, choir director at the Polatka Tabernacle House of Faith and Fire who, only moments before, had been flinging and waving her stout arms, leading everyone in song and jubilation right there at Danny's revival.

"Is the service over already?" I asked her.

"Oh, no honey, it ain't even close to being over. I always leave early. Gotta get to my other job." Her voice was rich, full of honey and brass. "Those folks can praise and carry on without me. I just get them started. I got money to earn, girl."

"Your other job?" I asked.

"Yeah, I sing at the roadhouse up the way. "Gator's Hideaway" it's called. A rowdy bunch of swamp critters, but praise God they do love this big ol' jiggly hunk o'woman belting out Johnny Cash and Willie Nelson tunes. Tips keep my kids in sneakers. Where you off to?"

"I don't know yet. All I know for now is that my mama was right—never marry a man who gets religion late," I opened the door and climbed in. She squealed off. The peal of the tires was lost in the peal of her great, hearty laughter.

"Lord, if we had just listened to our mamas! Help

yourself to a beer, baby. In the cooler behind the seat, underneath that choir robe. And open one for me, too. You know, we need a waitress down at the Hideaway."

Spa Interrupted

A WARM CLOTH IS PLACED over my eyes and I descend gently into a realm of touch and sound—bells tinkle, streams gurgle over smooth stones, birds chirp. Fingers play lightly over my body. Soft feathering touches arouse each nerve in eager anticipation of deeper probes and prods that will stimulate and remind my muscles of more supple times—tiny wires of tingling.

Lavender aroma coils its way up my nose. Hot oil drips on my forehead—soft liquid lava. Oxygen gusts on every pore of my face—a small Tinkerbell blowing tiny puffs through a miniature straw.

〰

Clusters of pale orange hibiscus drip lazily over huge terracotta pots. Palm trees whisper and play in the soft warm breeze, their curved trunks tethered to the earth by beds of bright purple peonies—sensual hula dancers.

A tiny changa, black and slick as oil, grooms himself with his sharp beak, then hops onto a green chair cushion, its scotch-guarded surface holding recent rain droplets in the shade. He sips daintily, yellow-rimmed, dark eyes darting everywhere at once.

A brigade of tropical colored casitas stands guard atop a cliff overlooking the translucent Caribbean Sea—a parade of pink, yellow and green fruit with white shutters and curved, orange tiled roofs undulate in the heat.

A sign on her large, white, wrought-iron cage reads, "My name is Cassie. I am a yellow headed Amazon. I am bilingual and have great wits." Her voice is cheerful, "Hello, Hola." She whistles softly, wraps her clawed feet tightly around her swing and pecks playfully at a suspended chain of small cork buoys and plastic toys, and cocks her head coyly.

A round, middle-aged bald man appears at the top of the Spanish tiled steps and surveys the pool—Don Quixote taking inventory of the windmills. His shirt is Hawaiian, open down the front, and reveals a massive chest of gray hair and several glistening gold chains. His baggy trunks are also Hawaiian—a different print. Turquoise rubber thongs hold him up, match his sunglasses. A saliva soaked cigar pokes through his clenched teeth.

The clack of high heels, red and strappy, a bronzed well-teased blonde emerges behind him. The tops of two round silicone breasts peek out of a red and white polka-dot bikini top, immobile despite the jingling and juggling of many brightly colored plastic bracelets.

"Tell me, Harry, how did you like your massage?" she asks him. He lumbers loudly down the steps, grabs the silver handrail, hurls himself into the pool—a great wallowing bull elephant heaving and grunting. Water splashes and rolls up over the sides.

The few swimmers slither out—sea snakes escaping a tidal wave. They find warmth and safety in sun-drenched lounge chairs.

"Well, sugar," he bellows above the splashing as his cigar bounces up and down, and ashes fly, "It was silly—all those crickets chirping and that hot greasy stuff dripping on my forehead."

He wipes at it, imagines it is still there.

"Why, Harry, that's your third eye," she hoots at him.

"My third eye? Hell, my other two ain't working so good, why did they wanna go and drown the third one?" They laugh raucously.

Harry trumpets a blaring discourse on spa treatments. "And that oxygen spitting on my face. Honey, you coulda just blown on it through one of those tiny drink straw—woulda cost a lot less. And you know I don't like guys touching me. 'Just keep your eyes closed and be in the moment,' that massage guy says to me. How could I be in the moment when I 'be' on a damned skinny table in a dark room?"

He sprays bits of spit, tobacco and New Age nonsense all at once.

Cassie begins to squawk and screech, and runs frantically back and forth on her perch. Her nervous, beady eyes rotate with every turn of her head.

Dishes clatter and clank in the kitchen behind the pool. A plate crashes onto the tile. A torrent of Spanish voices erupts, squabbling and cursing.

❦

An engine roars to life. The terrace cringes under the torrents of a power washer. A lawn mower revs on the grassy slope, its eager blades whirling and whining, preparing to attach the lush vegetation. The barking and bleating of a ferry horn tunnel up from the sea below. A plane thunders overhead, scarring the sky with its billowy exhaust. Palm fronds scrape and claw at one another, howling and tormented.

Harry floats on his back in the pool, his cigar pointing heavenward, his huge belly an emerging submarine. The blonde sits at the bar, straddling the bamboo bar stool, fluffing her hair and rubbing ice into her cleavage, while twirling and sucking noisily on a tiny, green paper umbrella she has removed from a tall, frothy, pink drink. Harry starts to snore.

Short Shorts

Snowmen fall from heaven unassembled.

= Unknown

Haunted

Eʟɪᴢᴀʙᴇᴛʜ ɴᴇᴠᴇʀ ʀᴇᴀʟʟʏ ᴡᴀɴᴛᴇᴅ to be a ghost. She had not given it much thought when she was alive. However, if someone had asked her what she would like to do in the afterlife, becoming a ghost would have been last on her list.

An angel, maybe. One that grabs young children when they are about to dash in front of an oncoming car, or a heavenly messenger sent to deliver soothing whispers to the dying, but a ghost? No, bottom of list.

So when she realized she had returned to the apartment where she spent the last ten years of her life, she was more than a little disappointed.

"I have no experience at this," she said aloud but heard nothing.

And of all the books still sitting on her bedside

table, "101 Easy Ways to Haunt," was not one of them.

Staring hard into the oval pine mirror attached to her dressing table, she saw nothing. She touched her face, gingerly at first, running her long dainty fingers down her cheeks, then roughly, smacking each one. Nothing. She could feel nothing.

"So, this is it," she said. "All a ghost has is awareness."

Obedience

THE LARGE, DRAB WAITING room was filled with dogs. They were circling, panting, sniffing, and pulling on leashes held tightly by their humans. A short, heavy, little bearded man in wrinkled khakis and a faded purple knit shirt sat on a straight backed chair in the corner. At the end of his leash stood a solemn, droop-mouthed bull dog. The man looked down at him.

"Sit," he commanded firmly.

Every dog in the room sat. You won't see that in a pediatrician's office.

Sportsmanship

WHEN KATHY'S OPPONENT RAMMED into her and knocked her painfully on her butt, her field hockey stick flew out of her hand. The whistle blew. A teammate pulled her slowly to her feet while offering the offending player a vicious smile.

"Watch your butt now, bitch," she snarled as the referee ran toward the three of them.

"Are you ok?" the ref looked at Kathy.

She remained silent for a few seconds, then answered, "Yeah, I think so." But the ref had already turned away.

Kathy rubbed her fanny, grinned at her teammate, and bent over to retrieve her stick. Grasping it firmly with two hands, she hefted it overhead and brought it down squarely on her opponent's head. The stick broke evenly and cleanly. As the girl hit the ground,

Kathy heard the referee's whistle again—this time louder.

Visionary

ONE SPRING DAY MY ninety year old neighbor looked out her kitchen window and gold gilded bird cages were flying through the air. Each one was lighted with tiny white sparkling lights.

Then she observed multi-colored tropical fish swimming through her shrubbery. She looked down and her sink began shattering and cracking.

"It is the Vioxx," her doctor said, unalarmed.

"Well, thank goodness I didn't see snakes or spiders," she told him.

Biking

HE WAS YOUNG, IN his twenties, handsome and hard-bodied. He guided me through the NordicTrack machines, one by one, showing me how adjust, add weights, squeeze, lift, pull up, push down, and every other contorted movement that could be made on them. He wrote it all down on a chart, to which I referred the next morning, confident I could climb aboard and become a well-built old body. I put myself in one. A middle aged T-shirted man lifting weights on the mat beside me gave me a huge smile. I smiled back.

"You're on that thing backwards," he said.

Lyrics

I HAD JUST LEARNED TO drive a four-speed. My brother still refused to let me behind the wheel of his car, so I had to be the passenger. The Buckinghams were singing "Kind of a Drag" on the radio. I sang along, loudly.

He looked over at me. "Kind of a Drag? I thought that was a Canada Dry commercial."

Ralphie

I HEARD HIM BEFORE HE came into view. He was a plump child, fat really, and his ample bottom and thighs crept perilously close to the edge of his large stroller seat. He was shouting loudly, talking to the haggard young woman pushing him.

I did not get the exact message he was trying to convey but he took the pacifier out of his mouth and punctuated the air with it each time he thought he had made a convincing point.

"Ralphie," his mother said wearily. "Aunt Sybil has gone to get your food. We are going to wait for her here. And she wheeled him directly in front of where I sat, plopping herself on the airport seat facing mine.

Ralphie looked at me. I quickly looked down at my book, praying he would not try to engage me in some nonsensical conversation. He became still. I peeked at him over my book. He was still staring right at me.

"Hi," I felt compelled to say.

He then produced a small purple ball from behind him on the stroller seat and hurled it directly at me. I instinctively raised my hand to shield my face. The ball bounced off my hand and rolled under my seat.

"Ralphie!" his mother scolded. He laughed. I leaned over and picked up his purple ball. Had she not been watching, I would have thrown it back at him. I handed it to her instead. Aunt Sybil returned with Burger King bags.

Living in Reverse

IF WE WERE BORN old, and we might as well be, considering old age requires the same caretaking upon which we were totally dependent when we were born—diapering and someone to care for our physical needs and our mental incapacity.

Our bodies and minds would become stronger as we approached middle age. The best part—we would have the knowledge, wisdom, and maturity of our forties, fifties, and sixties before we entered the incredibly difficult years of our youth. We could be sixteen and know that all the crap we are experiencing really doesn't matter. We would know that we are ok. Our abilities to deal with life and its unfairness and challenges would be firmly in place.

Then we could die happily on our tricycles while racing down the sidewalk. We could just enjoy our childhood and have fun, secure in ourselves because all the soul searching and self-journeying had taught us well.

Having learned our life's lessons and made it through our life's complications and challenges, we could just die peacefully in our cribs, having been rocked and sung to, cuddled and adored. And we would know what was going on.

Todos Santos

A HUMMINGBIRD APPEARED DIRECTLY IN front of my face; it hovered there, its wings beating frantically. I could see its little eyes looking at me. Right there on the sandy path back from the Pacific Ocean, whose pounding waves caused the earth to vibrate ever so slightly beneath my feet, I stopped.

"Who are you?" I asked the hummingbird. I got no answer but it lingered a minute more, staring at me. I thought it might be the spirit of someone I knew who had died. It wasn't long ago that I didn't know many people who had died. I can't say that anymore, as the years slip by.

Isn't that what some people think? Human spirits return in other forms. Wondering if it was my mother who died the previous year, I continued on up the path, taking care to watch for other critters that might not be as considerate as the hummingbird and slither right across my feet. It was the desert, after all. To the critters it belonged.

Baggage Claim

Airport baggage conveyors provide the ultimate setting for human beings displaying their true characters. A person watching for his suitcase knows no limits to pushing, shoving, grabbing, and slinging. Once he spies his own or what he thinks is his own container of soiled underwear, socks, wrinkled shirts and cheap, small trinkets to remind him of his journey somewhere, his focus wavers not.

Round and round the suitcases ride, some more woebegone than others. One spilled open just as it rounded the last corner, causing the goggling group of frowning travelers to stop shoving for a moment and ooh and aah at its pathetic offerings—a blue hairbrush peeking through a matted tangle of blonde hairs, several brightly colored strings connected to thin veils of nylon that were obviously thong under-

wear, and an assortment of muted, wrinkled, unidentifiable fabrics bundled and clinging to one another.
Then out rolled a crushed lime green and white mesh
Nike running shoe looking for its mate to make a
quick escape from the circle of onlookers.

The spilled contents elicited apparent empathy as
folks shook their heads and smiled. They were really
saying a silent prayer of thanks that the suitcase spitting out a life right there on the belt did not belong to
them. Not surprisingly, no one claimed it. On and on
it went. It is probably still going around now.

Landscape

TEMPERATURE RECORDS WERE BROKEN in mid-January at Virginia Beach where the boardwalk came alive with rollerbladers, skateboarders, dog walkers, stroller pushers, picture takers, scooter riders, bicyclists, people watchers, ice cream eaters, and joggers— not to mention rollerbladers pushing strollers, skateboarders walking dogs, picture takers watching people, bicyclists pulling scooter riders, joggers eating ice cream …. and folks sitting on benches watching all of the above.

How the nature of the landscape can be transformed by the teeming masses and all their contraptions!

Lawyer Times Two

Mr. reed did not realize he had awakened with two heads until he stumbled into the bathroom to shave and shower. Granted, he felt a bit heavier than usual when he tried to walk, but he told himself his head was still full of sleep. Until he looked in the mirror.

And there he was, Mr. Reed, attorney-at-law, father of two grown sons, and husband of plump and perky Mrs. Reed, with two heads. He was perplexed.

At that moment, his wife stepped into the bathroom and handed him his usual mug of morning coffee. Her pink plush velour robe was cinched as tight as it could be around her waist, given its girth. She looked first at her husband, then at his reflection.

"Oh, dear," she said, "I should have poured you two cups this morning. I'll go fetch another one."

She turned around and left. Mr. Reed just stood at the sink staring at his heads. Mrs. Reed returned shortly and handed him the second cup of coffee. Both of them peered into the mirror. Her brow furrowed. Both of his did, too.

"What am I going to do?" he asked and both of his mouths moved.

"Which one are you going to shave first is what I am wondering," his wife turned and touched first one face and then the other.

"Shave first?? What are you thinking?? How am I going to go to work?? What will I tell people?? What has happened to me??" his voice rose in exasperation.

"Oh my, I hadn't thought of that," Mrs. Reed put her hand under her chin and rolled her eyes. "Who in the world wants a two headed lawyer? Does this mean that each of your clients will get two wills, two property titles, two divorce agreements, two ...."

"Shut up!" his angry voice cut off her lilting listing. "This is serious."

"Why, of course it is, dear," she cooed. "Why don't you call the firm and tell them you are not feeling well today. Then we will sit down and discuss it."

Harvest

Moist summer heat rises from the black earth.
We pluck heavy red tomatoes from their vines,
Thick and ripe,
Bite into their firm flesh, smile.
Red juice squirts, joins with small seeds
Dribbling down our chins.
Lavender and rosemary toss their scents
Up our noses
Already tickled by swarming gnats
That we swat away.
I squat, gather sweet pungent basil leaves,
And ruffled heads of green lettuce.
My brown straw basket is heavy
With our twilight feast.
We will anoint our yield,
With biting balsamic vinegar,

Drink smooth, flinty Chablis.
Our lips will swell and pucker
Like they do when we kiss
Long and hard,
While your fingers play in the
Downy blonde hairs
At the small of my back.
You call softly for me to come to you.
We fall together in the lush fertile ground,
Savoring one another amid salty sweat
As it glistens on your face
And mingles with my tears.
They taste the same.
I open my eyes and look up at you,
A shimmering mirage in August air.
Our garden will cloy
As the last heavy tomatoes
Fall to the cooling, autumn earth in pulpy heaps.
And greens become brittle,
Their edges brown and turning in on themselves.
We gather our dirt-laden clothing,
Run inside for showers
To cleanse our bodies—
Lest your wife taste the sweetness,
Smell the bounty
Of our harvest—
As you tend hers.

Predator

I hate the scent, the sight, of dying
As the lions tear into the flesh of the shy water buffalo
Who had, seconds ago, been running, looking back
With terror as the hungry pride brought him down.
I wonder what it feels like to know that life is ending
Violently, painfully.
"The circle of life, every living thing must eat,"
My children tell me calmly, their cameras focused
On the noble, superior yellow-eyed stare of the predators
As their jaws drip warm succulent blood, filling the short space
Between the kill and our sturdy jeep with a
Raw, rusty, aroma—making me think of chickens, heads rolling
Under a broom handle, each end held tight by

My aunt's old lady black lace-up shoes
As she yanks their bodies off,
And tosses them in a heap where they wait
To be plucked and fried
For the farmhands' noon dinner.

Hurricane

She spews the ocean around,
Revs it up, slams it against shorelines
Without conscience.
Then the earth becomes a lullaby,
Calming her, hushing her.
She takes a last, lashing thrust,
Ensuring tumult.
Then swishes inland
Becoming as diminished
As a summer rainstorm,
Laughing over her shoulder
At the tumbled trees,
Befuddled power lines
And frenzied humans.
Rising water nips at her skirt
As she strolls off.

Does she look back
And sigh in her glory and her strength?
Or justify her violence
With the certainty
That we are arrogant in our humanity?

Obscurity

Is the sky really full of angels?
Do they bend an ear when a parent,
A child of God,
Created as the angels were—
By Him,
Scream in pain
For the death of a child?
Do they raise their white-robed fists in rage
When Satan pulls another of God's children
Into his dark abyss of drug addiction?
Or, do they weep celestial tears,
Turn their eyes heavenward
and ask their Creator,
"Why, why, why does the evil one
Have any power at all—
Now that Christ lived as man

And knew suffering and pain?
Or perhaps they have some understanding
Of how this universe works
That we do not have.
And that's why they are angels.

Genius is more often found in a cracked pot than in a whole one.

- E. B. White

ISBN 1425143628